CINDERELLA

and Other Tales by the Brothers Grimm

❧

CINDERELLA

AND OTHER TALES BY
THE BROTHERS GRIMM

JACOB AND
WILHELM GRIMM

Compiled and edited by Julia Simon-Kerr

▦ HarperFestival®
A Division of HarperCollins*Publishers*

The first collection of fairy tales
by the Brothers Grimm was published in 1812.

HarperCollins®, 🏠®, and HarperFestival®
are trademarks of HarperCollins Publishers Inc.

Cinderella and Other Tales by the Brothers Grimm
Printed in the United States of America.
All rights reserved.

For information address
HarperCollins Children's Books,
a division of HarperCollins Publishers,
1350 Avenue of the Americas,
New York, NY 10019.
www.harperchildrens.com

Library of Congress catalog card number: 2003116161

Typography by Fritz Metsch
3 4 5 6 7 8 9 10
❖
First HarperFestival edition, 2005

CONTENTS

*

CONTENTS

CINDERELLA

and Other Tales by the Brothers Grimm

✣

CINDERELLA

❖

NCE upon a time, there was a man, a widower, who took for his second wife a very proud woman.

This wife, a widow, had two daughters as proud as herself. Her husband had one daughter, who was gentle and good, as her own mother had been.

The new wife hated her young stepdaughter because her gentle ways and the sweetness of her temper, which was shown in her beautiful face, made the ill manners and frowning faces of her own daughters appear as disagreeable and ugly as they really were. So she set her to do all the meanest work of the house. The young girl swept, baked, and washed for the whole household. She wore only shabby clothes and slept in a bare garret.

NOW IT HAPPENED that the king's son made up his mind to give a ball, and to invite to it all the people of fashion in that countryside. There was to be dancing for two evenings, and the supper and entertainment were to be of a very splendid kind.

Cinderella's stepsisters were invited, and very proud and

happy they were, as they talked of the smart dresses they would wear and the grand folk they would meet at the palace.

When the great day came, Cinderella was busy from morning till evening, helping her stepsisters to get ready for the ball. She laced their gowns, dressed their hair, arranged their feathers and jewels, and even put on their slippers.

As she did so, they teased her to amuse themselves.

At last the sisters were ready and, with their mother, they drove away to the palace.

When they were gone, Cinderella, left alone, sat down among the cinders and began to cry.

When Cinderella looked up, she saw standing before her an old lady in a red cloak and pointed hat, leaning upon a stick. Cinderella was so much startled that she left off crying. This was Cinderella's godmother, who was a fairy.

"I can guess what you wish," said the fairy godmother. "You wish to go to the ball at the palace."

"Yes, indeed I do, dear godmother," cried Cinderella.

"Run into the garden," said the godmother, "and fetch me the largest pumpkin you can find."

Away went Cinderella, and very soon she ran back again, hugging a big green-and-yellow pumpkin.

The fairy godmother scooped out the inside of the pumpkin, leaving nothing but the rind. Then she touched it with her stick, which was really a fairy wand, and at once the pumpkin became a fine coach, shining all over with gold and lined with green.

"Now fetch the mousetrap," said she.

Cinderella obeyed quickly. In the mousetrap were six mice. The fairy godmother opened the trap, and as each mouse ran out, she touched it with her wand, and it became a sleek and prancing horse.

"There are your coach and horses," said she. "Now for the coachman. Bring me the rattrap."

Cinderella brought the rattrap. There were three rats in it. The fairy godmother chose the finest of the three and touched it with her wand. At once the rat became a tall and handsomely dressed coachman. "Behind the watering pot are six green lizards," said the fairy godmother. "Bring them here."

Cinderella brought the six lizards, and at a touch of the wand, each one was turned into a smart footman in a green uniform. The coachman mounted the box, and the footman climbed to the back of the coach. "Now your carriage is ready," said the fairy godmother.

"But how can I go to the ball like this?" said Cinderella, looking down at her shabby frock.

"You shall soon be more beautiful than your coach," replied her godmother, tapping Cinderella lightly with her wand. Then Cinderella's old clothes were turned into robes of silk and velvet, glittering with jewels. And the fairy godmother gave her a little pair of shining glass slippers, the prettiest that ever were seen.

"Remember," said her godmother, "you must leave the ball before the clock strikes twelve. If you do not, your coach will again become a pumpkin, your horses will become mice, your coachman will turn into a rat, and your footmen into lizards, while you will find yourself once more in shabby clothes."

As she entered the ball, the musicians ceased playing and the dancers stopped dancing, while all gazed in surprise at the lovely unknown princess.

All the evening, the prince kept at Cinderella's side, dancing with her and serving her with dainty dishes at suppertime. Indeed, his mind was so taken up with her that he forgot to eat a morsel himself. While Cinderella was talking to her stepsisters, who did not know it was Cinderella, the clock chimed a quarter before twelve. Cinderella rose, and after curtsying to the company, left the palace and drove home in her coach. Then she thanked her godmother for the kindness which had given her so much happiness, and asked leave to go to the ball again on the next evening, when the prince had specially begged her to come. At this moment there was a knock at the door. The fairy godmother and the beautiful clothes vanished as suddenly as they had appeared, and Cinderella drew back the bolt and let her stepmother and stepsisters in.

As she helped them off with their gowns, Cinderella's stepsisters couldn't stop talking of the beautiful princess who had been at the ball.

On the next evening, the stepsisters again went to the palace. And Cinderella went, too, in her coach, even more beautifully dressed than before. The prince again kept close beside her and said so many kind things to her that Cinderella in her happiness, forgot how quickly the hours flew past.

She thought it not yet eleven when the clock struck twelve. Then she started in fright and fled from the ballroom as swiftly as a deer. The prince ran after her, but he did not catch her. All he could find of her was a little glass slipper lying upon the staircase.

The next morning, folk were roused by a sound of trumpets; and through the streets of the town came the royal chamberlain, with guards and an attendant carrying the little glass slipper upon a velvet cushion.

Cinderella's stepsisters were desperate to try on the slipper. But, though they pinched their toes and squeezed their heels, their feet were far too large to fit into it. Then the royal chamberlain enquired whether there were any other young women in the house.

"Only Cinderella," said the elder sister. "Of course the slipper would not fit her."

"Let her be brought here," said the chamberlain.

So Cinderella was sent for, and, after she settled down in the chair, the royal chamberlain put the slipper on her foot.

Then, to the surprise of everyone, Cinderella drew the other little glass slipper from her pocket and put that on also. And at this moment the fairy godmother appeared and, with a touch of her wand, changed Cinderella's poor garments into robes, more splendid than ever.

And then everyone saw that she was indeed the beautiful princess whom the prince loved.

The stepsisters fell at Cinderella's feet and begged her forgiveness. And Cinderella freely forgave them and asked them to try to love her.

Then she was taken to the palace, where the prince met her with great joy, and married her.

Soon afterward, Cinderella fetched her stepsisters to live at the palace. They were so much ashamed of their past conduct, and so grateful for her kindness, that they ceased to be proud and unkind. And, as their hearts became good, their faces became beautiful. Then two lords of the court loved and married them, and they, as well as Cinderella, were happy.

RAPUNZEL

❊

HERE were once a man and a woman who had long in vain wished for a child. At length it seemed their wish would be granted. These people had a little window at the back of their house from which a splendid garden could be seen, which was full of the most beautiful flowers and herbs. It was, however, surrounded by a high wall, and no one dared to go into it because it belonged to an enchantress who had great power and was dreaded by all the world.

One day the woman was standing by this window and looking down into the garden when she saw a flowerbed planted with the most beautiful radish plants, called rapunzel. It looked so fresh and green that she longed for it, and had the greatest desire to eat some. This desire increased every day, and as she knew that she could not get any of it, she pined away and looked pale and miserable. Then her husband was alarmed, and asked, "What ails you, dear wife?"

"Ah," she replied, "if I can't get some of the rapunzel, which is in the garden behind our house, to eat, I shall die." The man, who loved her, thought to himself, *Sooner than let your wife die, bring her some of the rapunzel yourself, let it cost you what it will.*

In the twilight of the evening, he clambered down over the wall into the garden of the enchantress, hastily clutched a handful of rapunzel, and took it to his wife. She at once made herself a salad of it and ate it with much relish. She, however, liked it so very much that the next day she longed for it three times as much as before. If he was to have any rest, her husband must once more descend into the garden. In the gloom of evening, therefore, he let himself down again; but when he had clambered down the wall he was terribly afraid, for he saw the enchantress standing before him.

"How dare you descend into my garden and steal my rapunzel?" said she with an angry look. "You will suffer for it!"

"Ah," answered he, "let mercy take the place of justice, I only made up my mind to do it out of necessity. My wife saw your rapunzel from the window and felt such a longing for it that she would have died if she had not got some to eat."

Then the enchantress allowed her anger to be softened and said to him, "If the case be as you say, I will allow you to take away with you as much rapunzel as you wish. Only I make one condition, you must give me the child which your wife will bring into the world; it shall be well treated, and I will care for it like a mother." The man in his terror consented to everything, and when the woman gave birth to her child, the enchantress appeared at once, gave the child the name of Rapunzel, and took it away with her.

Rapunzel grew into the most beautiful child beneath the sun. When she was twelve years old, the enchantress shut her into a tower, which lay in a forest and had neither stairs nor a door, but only a little window quite at the top. When the enchantress wanted to go in, she placed herself beneath it and cried,

> *"Rapunzel, Rapunzel,*
> *Let down your hair."*

Rapunzel had magnificent long hair, fine as spun gold, and when she heard the voice of the enchantress she unfastened her braided tresses and wound them around one of the hooks of the window above. Then the hair fell seventy-five feet down, and the enchantress climbed up by it.

After a year or two, it came to pass that the king's son rode through the forest and went by the tower. Then he heard a song, which was so charming that he stood still and listened. This was Rapunzel, who in her solitude passed her time in letting her sweet voice resound. The king's son wanted to climb up to her and looked for the door of the tower, but none was to be found. He rode home, but the singing had so deeply touched his heart that every day he went out into the forest and listened to it. Once when he was thus standing behind a tree, he saw that an enchantress came there, and he heard how she cried,

> *"Rapunzel, Rapunzel,*
> *Let down your hair."*

Then Rapunzel let down the braids of her hair, and the enchantress climbed up to her. "If that is the ladder by which one ascends, I will for once try my fortune," said he. So the next day when it began to grow dark, he went to the tower and cried,

"Rapunzel, Rapunzel,
Let down your hair."

Immediately the hair fell down and the king's son climbed up.

At first Rapunzel was terribly frightened when a man, such as her eyes had never yet beheld, came to her; but the king's son began to talk to her quite like a friend and told her that his heart had been so stirred that it had let him have no rest, and he had been forced to see her. Then Rapunzel lost her fear, and when he asked her if she would take him for her husband, and she saw that he was young and handsome, she thought, *He will love me more than old Dame Gothel does.* And she said yes, and laid her hand in his.

She said, "I will willingly go away with you, but I do not know how to get down. Bring with you a skein of silk every time you come, and I will weave a ladder with it. When that is ready I will descend, and you will take me upon your horse."

They agreed that until that time he should come to her every evening, for the old woman came by day. The enchantress remarked nothing of this, until once Rapunzel said to her, "Tell me, Dame Gothel, how it happens that you are so much heavier for me to draw up than the king's young son—he is with me in a moment."

"Ah! you wicked child," cried the enchantress. "What do I hear you say! I thought I had separated you from all the world, and yet you have deceived me." In her anger she clutched Rapunzel's beautiful tresses, wrapped them twice around her left hand, seized a pair of scissors with the right, and snip, snap, they were cut off, and the lovely braids lay upon the ground. She was so heartless that she took poor Rapunzel into a desert where she had to live in great grief and misery.

On the same day that she cast out Rapunzel, the enchantress fastened the braids of hair which she had cut off to the hook of the window, and when the king's son came in the evening and cried,

"Rapunzel, Rapunzel,
Let down your hair, "

the enchantress let down the shorn hair. The king's son ascended, but he did not find his dearest Rapunzel above. Instead, the enchantress gazed at him with wicked and venomous looks. "Aha!" she cried mockingly. "You would fetch your dearest, but the beautiful bird sits no longer singing in the nest; the cat has got it, and will scratch out your eyes as well. Rapunzel is lost to you; you will never see her more."

The king's son was beside himself with pain, and in his despair he leapt down from the tower. He escaped with his life, but the thorns into which he fell pierced his eyes. Then he wandered quite blind about the forest, eating nothing but roots and berries and weeping over the loss of his dearest wife. Thus he roamed about in misery for some years, and at length came to the desert where Rapunzel lived in wretchedness. He heard a voice, and it seemed so familiar to him that he went toward it, and when he approached, Rapunzel recognized him and fell upon his neck and wept. Two of her tears wetted his eyes and they grew clear again, and he could see with them as before. He led her to his kingdom where he was joyfully received, and they lived for a long time afterward, happy and contented.

HANSEL AND GRETEL

✤

N the outskirts of a great forest dwelt a poor woodcutter with his wife and his two children. The boy was called Hansel and the girl, Gretel. Their mother had died and their father's new wife was cold and distant. The woodcutter had little to bite and to break, and once when a great famine fell upon the land, he could no longer procure even daily bread.

Now when he thought over this by night in his bed, and tossed about in his anxiety, he groaned and said to his wife, "What is to become of us? How are we to feed our poor children when we no longer have anything even for ourselves?"

"I'll tell you what, husband," answered the woman, "early tomorrow morning we will take the children out into the thickest part of the forest. There we will light a fire for them and give each of them one more piece of bread. After that we will go to our work and leave them alone. They will not find the way home again, and we shall be rid of them."

"No, wife," said the man, "I will not do that. How can I bear to leave my children alone in the forest? The wild animals would soon come and tear them to pieces."

"O you fool," said she, "then we must all four die of hunger, you may as well prepare the wood for our coffins," and she left him no peace until he consented.

"But I feel very sorry for the poor children, all the same," said the man. The two children had also not been able to sleep for hunger, and had heard what their stepmother had said to their father.

Gretel wept bitter tears and said to Hansel, "Now all is over with us."

"Be quiet, Gretel," said Hansel. "Do not distress yourself. I will soon find a way to help us."

And when the old folks had fallen asleep, he got up, put on his little coat, opened the door below, and crept outside. The moon shone brightly, and the white pebbles which lay in front of the house glittered like real silver coins. Hansel stooped and stuffed the little pocket of his coat with as many as he could fit. Then he went back and said to Gretel, "Be comforted, dear little sister, and sleep in peace. God will not forsake us," and he lay down again in his bed.

When day dawned but before the sun had risen, the woman came and awoke the two children, saying, "Get up, you sluggards. We are going into the forest to fetch wood." She gave each a little piece of bread and said, "There is something for your dinner, but do not eat it up before then, for you will get nothing else."

Gretel took the bread under her apron, as Hansel still had the pebbles in his pocket. Then they all set out together on the way to the forest. When they had walked a short time, Hansel stood still and peeped back at the house, then he did so again and again.

His father said, "Hansel, what are you looking at there and staying behind for? Pay attention, and do not forget how to use your legs."

"Ah, Father," said Hansel, "I am looking at my little white cat, which is sitting upon the roof and wants to say good-bye to me."

The wife said, "Fool, that is not your little cat, that is the morning sun shining upon the chimneys." Hansel, however, had not been looking back at the cat, but had been consistently dropping one of the white pebbles from his pocket onto the road.

When they had reached the middle of the forest, the father said, "Now, children, pile up some wood, and I will light a fire that you may not be cold." Hansel and Gretel gathered brushwood together, as high as a little hill.

The brushwood was lighted, and when the flames were burning very high, the woman said, "Now, children, lay yourselves down by the fire and rest, we will go into the forest and cut some wood. When we have done, we will come back and fetch you away."

Hansel and Gretel sat by the fire, and when noon came, each ate a little piece of bread, and as they heard the strokes of the wood-axe they believed that their father was near. It was not the axe, however, but a branch he had fastened to a withered tree that the wind was blowing backward and forward. Finally, they had been sitting such a long time that their eyes closed with fatigue and they fell fast asleep. When at last they awoke, it was already dark night.

Gretel began to cry and said, "How are we to get out of the forest now?"

But Hansel comforted her and said, "Just wait a little, until the moon has risen, and then we will soon find the way." And when the full moon had risen, Hansel took his little sister by the hand and followed the pebbles, which shone like newly coined silver pieces and showed them the way.

They walked the whole night long and by break of day came once more to their father's house. They knocked at the door, and when the woman opened it and saw that it was Hansel and Gretel, she said, "Naughty children, why have you slept so long in the forest? We thought you were never coming back at all." The father, however, rejoiced, for it had cut him to the heart to leave them behind alone.

Not long afterward, there was once more great famine throughout the land, and the children heard their mother saying at night to their father, "Everything is eaten again, we have only half a loaf of bread left, and that is the end. The children must go. We will take them farther into the wood, so that they will not find their way out again. There is no other means of saving ourselves." The man's heart was heavy, and he thought it would be better for him to share the last mouthful with his children.

The woman, however, would listen to nothing that he had to say, but scolded and reproached him. And just as he had yielded the first time, he did so again the second time.

The children, however, were still awake and had heard the conversation. When their parents were asleep, Hansel again got up to go out and pick up pebbles as he had done before, but the woman had locked the door and Hansel could not get out. Nevertheless, he comforted his little sister and said, "Do not cry, Gretel. Go to sleep quietly. I will think of something."

Early in the morning the woman came and took the children out of their beds. Their pieces of bread were given to them, but they were even smaller than the last time. On the way into the forest Hansel crumbled his in his pocket, and often stood still and threw a morsel upon the ground. "Hansel, why do you stop and look around?" asked the father.

"I am looking back at my little pigeon which is sitting upon the roof, and wants to say good-bye to me," answered Hansel.

"Fool," said the woman, "that is not your little pigeon, that is the morning sun shining on the chimney." Still, Hansel continued little by little to throw all the crumbs upon the path.

The woman led the children still deeper into the forest, where they had never in their lives been before. Then they again made a great fire, and the stepmother said, "Just sit there, children, and when you are tired you may sleep a little. We are going into the forest to cut wood, and in the evening when we are finished, we will come and fetch you away." When it was noon, Gretel shared her piece of bread with Hansel, who had scattered his by the way. Then they fell asleep and evening passed, but no one came to the poor children.

They did not awake until it was dark night, and Hansel comforted his little sister and said, "Just wait, Gretel, until the moon rises, and then we shall see the crumbs of bread which I have strewn about, and they will show us our way home again." When the moon came, they set out, but they found no crumbs, for the many thousands of birds that fly about in the woods and fields had eaten them all.

Hansel said to Gretel, "We shall soon find the way," but they did not find it. They walked the whole night and all the next day, too, from morning till evening, but they could not find the way out of the forest. They were very hungry, for they had nothing to eat but two or three berries, which grew upon the ground. When they were so weary that their legs would carry them no longer, they lay down beneath a tree and fell asleep.

It was now three mornings since they had left their father's house. They began to walk again, but they always came deeper into the forest, and they knew if help did not come soon, they must die of hunger and weariness. At midday on the third day, there suddenly appeared a beautiful snow-white bird sitting upon a bough. The bird sang so delightfully that Hansel and Gretel stood still and listened to it. When its song was over, it spread its wings and flew away before them, and they followed it until they reached a little house, upon the roof of which the bird had alighted. Hansel and Gretel's eyes opened wide with wonder for the house was built of bread and covered with cakes, and the windows were clear sugar.

"We will set to work on that," said Hansel, "and have a good meal. I will eat a bit of the roof, and you can eat some of the window. It will taste sweet." Hansel reached up and broke off a little of the roof to try how it tasted, and Gretel leaned against the window and nibbled at the panes.

All at once, a soft voice cried out from within the house,

"Nibble, nibble, gnaw,
Who is nibbling at my little house."

The children answered,

"The wind, the wind,
The whispering wind, "

and went on eating without disturbing themselves. Soon, they became greedy. Hansel, who liked the taste of the roof, tore down a great piece of it, and Gretel pushed out the whole of one round windowpane, then sat down to eat it. Suddenly the door opened, and a woman as old as the hills, who supported herself upon crutches, came creeping out. Hansel and Gretel were so terribly frightened that they let fall what they had in their hands.

The old woman, however, nodded her head and said, "Oh, you dear children, who has brought you here? Do come in, and stay with me. No harm shall happen to you." She took them both by the hand and led them into her little house. Then good food was set before them: milk and pancakes with sugar, apples, and nuts. Afterward, two pretty little beds were covered with clean, white linen, and Hansel and Gretel lay down in them and thought they were in heaven.

Poor Hansel and Gretel. The old woman had only pretended

to be so kind. She was in reality a wicked witch who lay in wait for children, and had only built the little house of sweets in order to entice children there. When a child fell into her power, she killed, cooked, and ate it, and had a feast. Witches have red eyes and cannot see far, but they have a keen scent like the beasts, and are aware when human beings draw near. Therefore, when Hansel and Gretel came into her neighborhood, she laughed with malice and said mockingly, "I have them, they shall not escape me again."

Early the next morning before the children were awake, she was already up, and when she saw both of them sleeping and looking so pretty with their plump and rosy cheeks, she muttered to herself, "That will be a dainty mouthful."

Then she seized Hansel with her shriveled hand, carried him into a little stable, and locked him in behind a grated door. Scream as he might, it would not help him. Next she went to Gretel, shook her till she awoke, and cried, "Get up, lazy thing, fetch some water, and cook something good for your brother. He is in the stable outside, and is to be made fat. When he is fat, I will eat him."

Gretel began to weep bitterly, but it was all in vain, for she was forced to do what the wicked witch commanded. And now the best food was cooked for poor Hansel. Gretel got nothing but crabshells.

Every morning the woman crept to the little stable and cried, "Hansel, stretch out your finger that I may feel if you will soon be fat!" Hansel, however, stretched out a little bone to her, and the old woman, who had dim eyes, could not see it and thought it was Hansel's finger, and was astonished that there was no way of fattening him.

When four weeks had gone by, and Hansel still remained thin, she was seized with impatience and would not wait any longer. "Now, then, Gretel," she cried to the girl, "stir yourself, and bring some water. Let Hansel be fat or lean, tomorrow I will kill him and cook him."

Ah, how the poor little sister did lament when she had to fetch the water, and how her tears did flow down her cheeks. "Dear God, do help us!" she cried. "If the wild beasts in the forest had but devoured us, we should at any rate have died together."

"Keep your noise to yourself," said the old woman. "It won't help you at all."

Early in the morning, Gretel had to go out and hang up the cauldron with the water and light the fire. "We will bake first," said the old woman. "I have already heated the oven and kneaded the dough."

She pushed poor Gretel out to the oven, from which flames of fire were already darting. "Creep in," said the witch, "and see if it properly heated so that we can put the bread in." And once Gretel was inside, she intended to shut the oven and let her bake in it, and then she would eat her, too.

But Gretel saw what the witch had in mind and said, "I do not know how I am to do it. How do I get in?"

"Silly goose," said the old woman, "the door is big enough. Just look, even I can get in," and she hobbled up and thrust her head inside the oven door. Then Gretel gave her a push that drove her far into the oven, shut the iron door, and fastened the bolt. The witch began to howl quite horribly, but

Gretel ran away, and the witch was miserably burnt to death.

Gretel immediately ran to Hansel, opened his little stable, and cried, "Hansel, we are saved! The old witch is dead!"

Then Hansel sprang like a bird from its cage when the door is opened. How they did rejoice and embrace each other and dance about! And as they had no longer any need to fear her, they went into the witch's house and found chests full of pearls and jewels in every corner .

"These are far better than pebbles," said Hansel, and thrust into his pockets whatever could be got in.

And Gretel said, "I, too, will take something home with me," and filled her pinafore full.

"But now we must be off," said Hansel, "that we may get out of the witch's forest."

When they had walked for two hours, they came to a great stretch of water.

"We cannot cross," said Hansel. "I see no footplank and no bridge."

"And there is also no ferry," answered Gretel, "but a white duck is swimming there. If I ask her, she will help us over." Then she cried,

> *"Little duck, little duck, do you see,*
> *Hansel and Gretel are waiting for you.*
> *There's never a plank, or bridge in sight,*
> *take us across on your back so white."*

The duck came to them, and Hansel seated himself upon its back and told his sister to sit by him. "No," replied Gretel, "that will be too heavy for the little duck. She shall take us across, one after the other."

The good little duck did so, and when they were safely across and had walked for a short time, the forest seemed to be more and more familiar to them, and at length they saw from afar their father's house. Then they began to run, rushed into the parlor, and threw themselves around their father's neck. The man had not known one happy hour since he had left the children in the forest, and in the meantime, his wife had died. Gretel emptied her pinafore until pearls and precious stones ran about the room, and Hansel threw one handful after another out of his pocket to add to them. Then all anxiety was at an end, and they lived together in perfect happiness.

TOM THUMB

✣

HERE was once a poor peasant who sat one evening by the hearth and poked the fire, while his wife sat and spun. "How sad it is that we have no children!" he said. With us all is so quiet, and in other houses it is noisy and lively."

"Yes," replied the wife, and sighed. "Even if we had only one, and it were quite small and only as big as a thumb, I should be quite satisfied, and we would still love it with all our hearts."

Now it so happened that the woman fell ill and after seven months gave birth to a child, who was perfect in all his limbs—but was no longer than a thumb.

Then said the man and his wife, "He is just as we wished him to be, and he shall be our dear child;" and because of his size, they called him Tom Thumb.

They did not let him want for food, but the child did not grow taller and remained as he had been at the first. Nevertheless, he looked intelligently at the world and soon showed himself to be a wise and nimble creature, for everything he did turned out well.

One day, the peasant was getting ready to go into the forest to cut wood, when he said as if to himself, "How I wish that there was anyone who would bring the cart to me!"

"Oh, Father!" cried Tom Thumb. "I will soon bring the cart, rely on that; it shall be in the forest at the appointed time."

The man smiled and said, "How can that be done? You are far too small to lead the horse by the reins."

"That's of no consequence, Father, if my mother will only harness it, I shall sit in the horse's ear and call out to him how he is to go."

"Well," answered the man, "for once we will try it."

When the time came, the mother harnessed the horse and placed Tom Thumb in its ear, and then the little creature cried, "Gee up, gee up!"

Then it went quite properly as if with its master, and the cart went the right way into the forest. It so happened that just as the horse was turning a corner, and the little one was crying, "Gee up," two strange men came toward him.

"My word!" said one of them. "What is this? There is a cart coming, and a driver is calling to the horse and still he is not to be seen!"

"That can't be right," said the other. "We will follow the cart and see where it stops." The cart, however, drove right into the forest and exactly to the place where the wood had been cut. When Tom Thumb saw his father, he cried to him, "Look, Father, here I am with the cart; now take me down." The father got hold of the horse with his left hand and with the right took his little son out of its ear. Tom Thumb sat down quite merrily upon a straw, but when the two strange men saw him, they did not know what to say for astonishment. Then one of them took the other aside and said, "Hark, the little fellow would make our fortune if we exhibited him in a large town for money. We will buy him."

They went to the peasant and said, "Sell us the little man. He shall be well treated with us."

"No," replied the father, "he is the apple of my eye, and all the money in the world could not buy him from me."

Tom Thumb, however, when he heard of the bargain, had crept up the folds of his father's coat, placed himself upon his shoulder, and whispered in his ear, "Father, do give me away. I will soon come back again." So the father parted with him to the two men for a handsome bit of money.

"Where would you like to sit?" they said to him.

"Oh, just set me upon the rim of your hat, and then I can walk backward and forward and look at the country, and still not fall down."

They did as he wished, and when Tom Thumb had taken leave of his father, they went away with him. They walked until it was dusk, and then the little fellow said, "Do take me down. I want to come down!" The man hesitated at first, but finally took his hat off and put the little fellow upon the ground by the wayside. Tom Thumb crept about a little between the sods, until suddenly he slipped into a mousehole he had found. "Good evening, gentlemen, just go home without me!" he cried, laughing. The two men ran thither and stuck their sticks into the mousehole, but it was in vain. Tom

Thumb crept still farther in, and as it soon became quite dark, the men were forced to go home with their vexation and their empty purses.

When Tom Thumb saw that they were gone, he crept back out of the subterranean passage. "It is so dangerous to walk on the ground in the dark," said he; "how easily a neck or a leg is broken!" Fortunately he knocked against an empty snail shell. "Thank God!" said he. "In that I can pass the night in safety," and he got into it.

Not long afterward, when he was just going to sleep, he heard two men go by, and one of them was saying, "How shall we contrive to get hold of the rich pastor's silver and gold?"

"I could tell you that," cried Tom Thumb, interrupting them.

"What was that?" said one of the thieves in fright. "I heard someone speaking." They stood still listening, and Tom Thumb spoke again, and said, "Take me with you, and I'll help you."

"But where are you?"

"Just look on the ground and follow my voice," he replied. There the thieves at length found him and lifted him up. "You little imp, how can you help us?" they said.

"A great deal," said he. "I will creep into the pastor's room through the iron bars, and will pass out to you whatever you want to have."

"Come then," they said, "and we will see what you can do."

When they got to the pastor's house, Tom Thumb crept into the room, but instantly cried out with all his might,

"Do you want to have everything that is here?" The thieves were alarmed and said, "But do speak softly, so as not to waken anyone!"

Tom Thumb, however, behaved as if he had not understood this, and cried again, "What do you want? Do you want to have everything that is here?" The cook, who slept in the next room, heard this and sat up in bed, and listened.

The thieves, however, had, in their fright, run some distance away, but at last they took courage, and thought, *The little rascal wants to mock us.* They came back and whispered to him, "Come, be serious, and hand something out to us."

Then Tom Thumb again cried as loudly as he could, "I really will give you everything, just put your hands in."

The maid, who was listening, heard this quite distinctly, and jumped out of bed and rushed to the door. At the same time, the thieves took flight and ran as if the Wild Huntsman were behind them. As the maid could not see anything, she went to strike a light. By the time she came back with it, Tom Thumb, unperceived, had gone and hid himself in the granary. After she had examined every corner and found nothing, the maid lay down in her bed again, and believed that, after all, she had only been dreaming with open eyes and ears.

Tom Thumb had climbed up among the hay and found a beautiful place to sleep; there he intended to rest until day, and then go home again to his parents. But there were other adventures in store for him. Truly, there is much affliction and misery in this world!

When day dawned, the maid arose from her bed to feed the cows. Her first step was to go into the barn and secure an armful of hay. Alas! It was precisely that very one in which poor Tom Thumb was lying asleep. He, however, was sleeping so soundly that he was aware of nothing and did not awake until he was in the mouth of the cow, who had picked him up with the hay.

"Ah, heavens!" cried he. "How have I got into the grinding mill?" But he soon realized where he was and was careful not to let himself get between the teeth and be crushed. Finally, he slipped down into the stomach with the hay. "In this little room the windows are forgotten," said he, "and no sun shines in, neither will a candle be brought."

His quarters were especially unpleasing to him, and the worst was, more and more hay was always coming in by the door, and the space grew less and less.

At length in his anguish, he cried as loud as he could, "Bring me no more fodder, bring me no more fodder!"

The maid was just milking the cow, and when she heard someone speaking but saw no one, she perceived that it was the same voice that she had heard in the night and was so terrified that she slipped off her stool and spilt the milk. She ran in great haste to her master and said, "Oh heavens, pastor, the cow has been speaking!"

"You are mad," replied the pastor; but he went himself to the barn to see what was there. Hardly, however, had he set his foot inside when Tom Thumb again cried, "Bring me no more fodder, bring me no more fodder!" Then the pastor himself was alarmed, and thought that an evil spirit had gone into the cow and ordered her to be killed. So the cow was killed, and the stomach, in which Tom Thumb was trapped, was thrown on the dung heap. Tom Thumb had great difficulty in working his way out. Finally, just as he was almost free, a new misfortune occurred. A hungry wolf found the dung heap and swallowed the whole stomach at one gulp. Tom Thumb did not lose courage. *Perhaps,* thought he, *the wolf will listen to what I have to say,* and he called to him from out of his stomach, "Dear wolf, I know of a magnificent feast for you!"

"Where is it to be had?" said the wolf.

"In such and such a house. You must creep into it through the kitchen drain, and there you will find as much cakes, bacon, and sausages as you can eat," and he described to him exactly his father's house. The wolf did not need to be told twice. He squeezed himself in at night through the drain, and ate to his heart's content in the larder. When he had eaten his fill, he wanted to go out again, but he had become so big that he could not go out by the same way. Tom Thumb had reckoned on this, and now began to make a violent noise in the wolf's body, and raged and screamed as loudly as he could.

"Will you be quiet," said the wolf. "You will wake up the people!"

"Eh, what," replied the little fellow, "you have eaten your fill, and I will make merry likewise," and he began once more to scream with all his strength. At last his father and mother were aroused by it, and ran to the room and looked in through the opening in the door. When they saw that a wolf was inside, they ran away, and the husband fetched his axe, and the wife the scythe. "Stay behind," said the man when they entered the room. "When I have given him a blow, if he is not killed by it, you must cut him down and hew his body to pieces."

Then Tom Thumb heard his parents' voices and cried, "Dear Father, I am here! I am in the wolf's body!"

Said the father, full of joy, "Thank God, our dear child has found us again," and bade the woman take away her scythe, that Tom Thumb might not be hurt with it. After that he raised his arm and struck the wolf such a blow upon his head that he fell down dead. Then they got knives and scissors and cut his body open and drew the little fellow forth.

"Ah," said the father, "what sorrow we have gone through for your sake."

"Yes, Father, I have gone about the world a great deal. Thank heaven, I breathe fresh air again!"

"Where have you been, then?"

"Ah, Father, I have been in a mouse's hole, in a cow's stomach, and then in a wolf's; now I will stay with you."

"And we will not sell you again, no, not for all the riches in the world," said his parents, and they embraced and kissed their dear Tom Thumb. Then they gave him food to eat and drink, and had some new clothes made for him, for his own had been spoiled on his journey.

LITTLE RED RIDING HOOD

❖

NCE upon a time there was a dear little girl who was loved by everyone who looked at her, but most of all by her grandmother. There was nothing that her grandmother would not have given to the child. Once she gave her a little cap of red velvet, which suited the girl so well that she would never wear anything else; from then on she was always called "Little Red Riding Hood."

One day her mother said to her, "Come, Little Red Riding Hood, here is a piece of cake and a bottle of wine; take them to your grandmother. She is ill and weak, and they will do her good. Set out before it gets hot, and when you are going, walk nicely and quietly and do not run off the path, or you may fall and break the bottle. Then your grandmother will get nothing. And when you go into her room, don't forget to say, 'Good morning,' and don't peep into every corner before you do it."

"I will take great care," said Little Red Riding Hood to her mother, and gave her hand on it.

The grandmother lived out in the wood, half a league from the village. Just as Little Red Riding Hood entered the wood, she saw a wolf. Little Red Riding Hood did not know what a wicked creature he was, and was not at all afraid of him.

"Good day, Little Red Riding Hood," said he.

"Thank you kindly, wolf."

"Where are you off to so early, Little Red Riding Hood?"

"To my grandmother's."

"What have you got in your apron?"

"Cake and wine; yesterday was baking day, so poor, sick Grandmother is to have something good, to make her stronger."

"Where does your grandmother live, Little Red Riding Hood?"

"A good quarter of a league farther on into the wood; her house stands under the three large oak trees and next to the hazelnut bushes; surely you must know it," replied Little Red Riding Hood.

The wolf thought to himself, *What a tender young creature! What a nice plump mouthful—she will be better to eat than the old woman. I must act craftily, so as to catch both.* So he walked for a short time by the side of Little Red Riding Hood, and then he said, "See, Little Red Riding Hood, how pretty the flowers are about here—why do you not look around? I believe, too, that you do not hear how sweetly the little birds are singing. You walk gravely along as if you were going to school, while everything else out here in the wood is merry."

Little Red Riding Hood raised her eyes, and when she saw the sunbeams dancing here and there through the trees, and pretty flowers growing everywhere, she thought, *Suppose I take Grandmother a fresh nosegay; that would please her, too. It is so early in the day that I shall still get there in good time;* and so she ran from the path into the wood to look for flowers. And whenever she had picked one, she fancied that she saw a still prettier one farther on and ran after it, and so got deeper and deeper into the wood.

Meanwhile, the wolf ran straight to the grandmother's house and knocked at the door.

"Who is there?"

"Little Red Riding Hood," replied the wolf, "bringing cake and wine. Open the door."

"Lift the latch," called out the grandmother. "I am too weak, and cannot get up."

The wolf lifted the latch and the door flew open. Then, without saying a word, he went straight to the grandmother's bed, and devoured her. When he was finished, he put on her clothes, dressed himself in her cap, laid himself in bed, and drew the curtains.

Little Red Riding Hood, meanwhile, had been running about picking flowers, and when she had gathered so many that she could carry no more, she remembered her grandmother and set out upon the way to her.

She was surprised to find the cottage door standing open, and when she went into the room, she had such a strange feeling that she said to herself, "Oh, dear! How uneasy I feel today, and at other times I look forward to being with Grandmother so much." She called out, "Good morning!" But she received no answer. Then she went to the bed and drew back the curtains. There lay her grandmother with her cap pulled far over her face, looking very strange.

"Oh! Grandmother," she said, "what big ears you have!"

"The better to hear you with, my child," was the reply.

"But, Grandmother, what big eyes you have!" she said.

"The better to see you with, my dear."

"But, Grandmother, what large hands you have!"

"The better to hug you with."

"Oh! But, Grandmother, what a terrible big mouth you have!"

"The better to eat you with!"

And scarcely had the wolf said this, than with one bound he was out of bed and had swallowed up Little Red Riding Hood.

When the wolf had appeased his appetite, he lay down again in the bed, fell asleep, and began to snore very loud. Just then a huntsman was passing the house and thought to himself, *How the old woman is snoring! I must just see if she wants anything.* So he went into the room, and when he came to the bed, he saw that the wolf was lying in it.

"Do I find you here, you old sinner!" said he. "I have long sought you!" Then, just as he was going to fire at him, it occurred to him that the wolf might have devoured the grandmother and that she might still be saved. So he did not fire, but instead took a pair of scissors and began to cut open the stomach of the sleeping wolf. When he had made two snips, he saw a little red hood shining. Then he made two snips more, and the little girl sprang out, crying, "Ah, how frightened I have been! How dark it was inside the wolf!"

After that the aged grandmother came out alive also, but scarcely able to breathe. Little Red Riding Hood quickly fetched great stones with which they filled the wolf's body, and when he awoke, he wanted to run away, but the stones were so heavy that he fell down at once, and was dead.

Then all three were delighted. The huntsman drew off the wolf's skin and went home with it; the grandmother ate the cake and drank the wine that Little Red Riding Hood had brought, and was revived. Little Red Riding Hood thought to herself, *As long as I live, I will never by myself leave the path to run into the wood when my mother has forbidden me to do so.*

IT IS ALSO related that once when Little Red Riding Hood was again taking cakes to her grandmother, another wolf spoke to her and tried to entice her from the path. Little Red Riding Hood, however, was on her guard and went straight forward upon her way. She told her grandmother that she had met another wolf, that he had said good morning to her—but with such a wicked look in his eyes that, if they had not been on the public road, she was certain he would have eaten her up. "Well," said the grandmother, "we will shut the door, that he may not come in." Soon afterward the wolf knocked and cried, "Open the door, Grandmother! I am Little Red Riding Hood, and am bringing you some cakes!" But they did not speak or open the door. The wolf stole twice or thrice around the house and at last jumped upon the roof, intending to wait until Little Red Riding Hood went home in the evening, then to steal after her and devour her in the darkness. But the grandmother saw what was in his thoughts. In front of the house was a great stone trough, so she said to the child, "Take the pail, Little Red Riding Hood. I made some sausages yesterday. Carry the water in which I boiled them to the trough." Little Red Riding Hood carried water until the great trough was quite full. The smell of the sausages reached the wolf, and he sniffed and peeped down. He stretched out his neck so far that he could no longer keep his footing and began to slip. At last, he slipped down from the roof straight into the great trough and was drowned. Little Red Riding Hood went joyously home and was never harmed by anyone.

SLEEPING BEAUTY

᠅

LONG time ago, there lived a king and queen who said every day, "Ah, if only we had a child!" but they never had one.

Then one day, when the queen was bathing, a frog crept out of the water onto the land and said to her, "Your wish shall be fulfilled. Before a year has gone by, you shall have a daughter."

What the frog had said came true, and the queen had a little girl who was so pretty that the king could not contain himself for joy and ordered a great feast. He invited not only his kindred, friends, and acquaintances, but also the Wise Women, in order that they might be kind and well-disposed toward the child. There were thirteen Wise Women in his kingdom, but, as he had only twelve golden plates for them to eat out of, one of them had to be left at home.

The feast was held with all manner of splendor. When it came to an end the Wise Women bestowed their magic gifts upon the baby: one gave virtue, another beauty, a third riches, and so on until she had been given everything in the world that one can wish for.

When eleven of the Wise Women had made their promises, the thirteenth suddenly entered. She wished to avenge herself for not having been invited, and without greeting or even looking at anyone, she cried with a loud voice, "The king's daughter shall in her fifteenth year prick herself with a spindle and fall down dead!" And, without saying a word more, she turned around and left the room.

They were all shocked; but the twelfth Wise Woman, whose good wish still remained unspoken, came forward. She could not undo the evil sentence, only soften it, so she said, "It shall not be death, but a deep sleep of a hundred years, into which the princess shall fall."

The king, who would fain keep his dear child from the misfortune, gave orders that every spindle in the whole kingdom should be burnt. Meanwhile, the gifts of the Wise Women were plentifully bestowed. The young girl was so beautiful, modest, good-natured, and wise that everyone who saw her was bound to love her.

Now it happened that upon the very day when the princess was fifteen years old the king and queen were not at home, and the maiden was left in the palace quite alone. So she went exploring into all sorts of places, looked into rooms and bedchambers just as she liked, and at last came to an old tower. She climbed up the narrow winding staircase and reached a little door. A rusty key was in the lock, and when she turned it the door sprang open, and there in a little room sat an old woman with a spindle, busily spinning her flax.

"Good day, old dame," said the king's daughter. "What are you doing there?"

"I am spinning," said the old woman, and nodded her head.

"What sort of thing is that, that rattles around so merrily?" said the girl, and she took the spindle and wanted to spin, too. But scarcely had she touched the spindle when the magic decree was fulfilled, and she pricked her finger with it.

And, in the very moment when she felt the prick, she fell down upon the bed that stood there and lay in a deep sleep. This sleep extended over the whole palace. The king and queen, who had just come home and had entered the great hall, began to go to sleep, and the whole of the court with them. The horses, too, went to sleep in the stable, the dogs in the yard, the pigeons upon the roof, the flies upon the wall; even the fire that was flaming upon the hearth became quiet and slept, the roast meat left off sizzling, and the cook, who was just going to pull the hair of the scullery boy because he had forgotten something, let him go and went to sleep. The wind fell, and upon the trees before the castle not a leaf moved again.

Soon around the castle there began to grow a hedge of thorns. Every year it became higher, until at last it grew close up around the castle and all over it, so that there was nothing of it to be seen, not even the flag upon the roof. The story of the beautiful Sleeping Beauty—for so the princess was named—went about the country, so that from time to time kings' sons came and tried to get through the thorny hedge into the castle.

But they found it impossible, for the thorns held fast together, as if they had hands. The youths got caught in them, could not get loose again, and died miserable deaths.

After many, many years a king's son came again to that

country. He had heard an old man talking about the thorn-hedge, and about a castle that was said to stand behind it, in which a wonderfully beautiful princess named Sleeping Beauty had been asleep for a hundred years, along with the king and queen and the whole court. The old man had heard, too, from his grandfather that many kings' sons had already come and had tried to get through the thorny hedge, but they had remained sticking fast in it and had died a pitiful death.

When he heard this, the youth said, "I am not afraid, I will go and see the beautiful Sleeping Beauty." The good old man tried hard to dissuade him, but the king's son did not listen to his words.

Now at this time the hundred years had just passed, and the day had come when Sleeping Beauty was to awaken again. When the king's son came near to the thornhedge, it was nothing but large and beautiful flowers, which parted from one another of their own accord and let him pass unhurt, then closed again behind him like a hedge. In the castle yard he saw the horses and the spotted hounds lying asleep; upon the roof sat the pigeons with their heads under their wings. And when he entered the house, the flies were asleep upon the wall, the cook in the kitchen was still holding out his hand to seize the boy, and the maid was sitting by the black hen which she had been going to pluck.

He went on farther, and in the great hall he saw the whole of the court lying asleep, and up by the throne lay the king and queen.

Then he went on still farther, and all was so quiet that a breath could be heard. At last he came to the tower and opened the door into the little room where Sleeping Beauty was sleeping. There she lay, so beautiful that he could not turn his eyes away; and he stooped down and gave her a kiss. As soon as he kissed her, Sleeping Beauty opened her eyes, awoke, and looked at him quite fondly.

Then the two went downstairs together, and the king and the queen awoke, along with the whole court, and they looked at each other in great astonishment. The horses in the court-yard stood up and shook themselves; the hounds jumped up and wagged their tails; the pigeons upon the roof pulled out their heads from under their wings, looked around, and flew into the open country; the flies upon the wall crept again; the fire in the kitchen burned up and flickered and cooked the meat; the joint began to turn and sizzle again, and the cook gave the boy such a box on the ear that he screamed, and the maid plucked the fowl ready for the spit.

The marriage of the king's son with Sleeping Beauty was celebrated with all splendor, and they lived contented to the end of their days.

THE FROG-PRINCE

❦

I N olden times, when wishing still helped, there lived a king whose daughters were all beautiful. But the youngest was so beautiful that the sun itself, which has seen so much, was astonished whenever it shone upon her face. Close by the king's castle lay a great dark forest, and under an old lime tree in the forest was a well. When the day was very warm, the king's child went out into the forest and sat down by the side of the cool fountain, and when she was dull she took a golden ball. This ball was her favorite plaything. She would throw it into the air and then catch it again. She loved this ball more than anything else.

Now it so happened that upon one occasion the princess's golden ball did not fall into the little hand which she was holding up for it, but onto the ground beyond, where it rolled straight into the water. The king's daughter followed it with her eyes, but it vanished, for the well was deep, so deep that the bottom could not be seen. She began to cry, and she cried louder and louder, and could not be comforted. As she thus lamented, a voice said to her, "What ails you, king's daughter? You weep so that even a stone would show pity." The princess looked around to the side from whence the voice came, and saw a frog stretching forth its thick, ugly head from the water. "Ah! Old water-splasher, is it you?" said she. "I am weeping for my golden ball, which has fallen into the well."

"Be quiet, and do not weep," answered the frog. "I can help you, but what will you give me if I bring your plaything up again?"

"Whatever you will have, dear frog," said she. "My clothes, my pearls and jewels, and even the golden crown which I am wearing."

The frog answered, "I do not care for your clothes, your pearls and jewels, or your golden crown. But if you will love me and let me be your companion and playfellow, and sit by you at your little table, and eat off your little golden plate, and drink out of your little cup, and sleep in your little bed—if you will promise me this, I will go down below and bring you your golden ball up again."

"Oh, yes," said she, "I promise you all you wish, if you will but bring me my ball back again." She, however, thought, *How that silly frog does talk! He lives in the water with the other frogs, and croaks, and can be no companion to any human being!*

But the frog, when he had received this promise, put his head into the water and sank down. In a short while, he came swimming up again with the ball in his mouth and threw it upon the grass. The king's daughter was delighted to see her pretty plaything once more, picked it up, and ran away with it. "Wait, wait!" said the frog. "Take me with you! I can't run as you can!" But what did it avail him to *croak* after her as loudly as he could? She did not listen to it, but ran home and soon forgot the poor frog, who was forced to go back into his well again.

The next day, when she had seated herself at table with the king and all the courtiers, and was eating from her little golden plate, something came creeping, *splish-splash, splish-splash*, up the marble staircase. When it had gotten to the top, it knocked at the door and cried, "Princess, youngest princess, open the door for me." She ran to see who was outside, but when she opened the door, there sat the frog in front of it. She slammed the door in great haste, sat down to dinner again, and was quite frightened. The king saw plainly that her heart was beating violently and said, "My child, what are you so afraid of? Is there perchance a giant outside who wants to carry you away?"

"Ah, no," replied she. "It is no giant, but a disgusting frog."

"What does a frog want with you?"

"Ah, dear Father, yesterday as I was in the forest sitting by the well, playing, my golden ball fell into the water. And because I cried so, the frog brought it out again for me, and because he so insisted, I promised him he should be my companion. But I never thought he would be able to come out of his water! And now he is outside there and wants to come in to me."

In the meantime the frog knocked a second time and cried,

> *"Princess! youngest princess!*
> *Open the door for me!*
> *Have you forgotten what you promised me*
> *Yesterday by the cool waters of the fountain?*
> *Princess, youngest princess!*
> *Open the door for me!"*

Then said the king, "That which you have promised you must perform. Go and let him in." She went and opened the door, and the frog hopped in and followed her, step by step, to her chair. There he sat and cried, "Lift me up beside you!"

She delayed, until at last the king commanded her to do it. When the frog was on the chair he wanted to be upon the table. And when he was upon the table he said, "Now, push your little golden plate nearer to me so that we may eat together." She did this, but it was easy to see that she did not do it willingly. The frog enjoyed what he ate, but almost every mouthful she took choked her. At length he said, "I have eaten and am satisfied; now I am tired. Carry me into your little room and make your little silken bed ready, and we will both lie down and go to sleep."

The king's daughter began to cry, for she was afraid of the cold frog which she did not like to touch and which was now to sleep in her pretty, clean little bed. But the king grew angry and said, "He who helped you when you were in trouble ought not afterward to be despised by you."

So she took hold of the frog with two fingers, carried him upstairs, and put him in a corner. But when she was in bed he crept to her and said, "I am tired, I want to sleep as well as you. Lift me up or I will tell your father." Then she was terribly angry, and took him up and threw him with all her might against the wall. "Now, you will be quiet, odious frog," said she.

But when he fell down he was no longer a frog, but a king's son with beautiful, kind eyes. And, as was her father's will, she accepted him as her dear companion and husband. Then he told her how he had been bewitched by a wicked witch and how no one could have delivered him from the well but herself, and that tomorrow they would go together into his kingdom.

Then they went to sleep. The next morning when the sun awoke them, a carriage came driving up with eight white horses. The horses had white ostrich feathers on their heads, and were harnessed with golden chains. Behind them stood the young king's servant, Faithful Henry. Faithful Henry had been so unhappy when his master was changed into a frog that he had caused three iron bands to be laid around his heart, lest it should burst with grief and sadness.

The carriage was to conduct the young king into his kingdom. Faithful Henry helped them both in and placed himself behind again, full of joy because of this deliverance. And when they had driven a part of the way the king's son heard a cracking behind him as if something had broken. So he turned around and cried, "Henry, the carriage is breaking!"

"No, master, it is not the carriage. It is a band from my heart, which was put there in my great pain when you were a frog and imprisoned in the well." Again and once again while they were on their way, something cracked, and each time the king's son thought the carriage was breaking. But it was only the bands which were springing from the heart of Faithful Henry because his master was set free and was happy.

SNOW WHITE

❧

NCE upon a time in the middle of winter, when flakes of snow were falling like feathers from the sky, a queen sat sewing at a window with a black ebony frame. While she was sewing and looking out of the window at the snow, she pricked her finger with the needle, and three drops of blood fell upon the snow. The red looked pretty upon the white snow, and she thought to herself, "Would that I had a child as white as snow, as red as blood, and as black as the wood of the window-frame."

Soon after that, she had a little daughter who was as white as snow, with lips as red as blood, and whose hair was as black as ebony. She was therefore called little Snow White. Alas, when the child was born, the queen died.

After a year had passed, the king took to himself another wife. She was a beautiful woman, but proud and haughty, and she could not bear that anyone else should surpass her in beauty. She had a wonderful looking glass, and when she stood in front of it and looked at herself in it, she said,

"Mirror, mirror, on the wall,
Who in this land is the fairest of all?"

Then the looking glass would answer,

"You, O Queen, are the fairest of all!"

Then she was satisfied, for she knew that the looking glass spoke the truth.

But Snow White was growing up and becoming more and more beautiful. When she reached seven years old, she was as beautiful as the day, more beautiful than the queen herself. Then, when the queen asked her looking glass,

"Mirror, mirror, on the wall,
Who in this land is the fairest of all?"

it answered,

"You are fairer than most, 'tis true.
But fairer still is Snow White than you!"

Then the queen was shocked and turned yellow and green with envy. From that hour, whenever she looked at Snow White, her heart heaved in her breast with the force of her hatred.

Gradually, envy and pride grew higher and higher in her heart like a weed so that she had no peace, day or night. Until one day she called a huntsman and said, "Take the child away into the forest; I will no longer have her in my sight. Kill her, and bring me back her heart as a token."

The huntsman obeyed and took Snow White away. But when he had drawn his knife and was about to pierce Snow White's innocent heart, she began to weep and said, "Ah, dear huntsman, leave me my life! I will run away into the wild forest and never come home again."

As she was so beautiful, the huntsman pitied her and said, "Run away, then, you poor child." *The wild beasts will soon have devoured you*, thought he. Yet it seemed as if a stone had been rolled from his heart since it was no longer needful for him to kill her. A young boar just then came running by and he stabbed it, cut out its heart, and took it to the queen as proof that the child was dead. The cook had to salt this, and the wicked queen ate it, believing that she had eaten the heart of Snow White.

But now the poor child was all alone in the great forest, and so terrified that she looked at every leaf of every tree and did not know what to do. Then she began to run, and ran over sharp stones and through thorns. The wild beasts ran past her, but did her no harm.

She ran as long as her feet would go until it was almost evening; then she saw a little cottage and went into it to rest herself. Everything in the cottage was small, but neater and cleaner than can be told. There was a table upon which was a white cover and seven little plates, and upon each plate a little spoon; moreover, there were seven little knives and forks, and seven little mugs. Against the wall stood seven little beds side by side, covered with sheets as white as snow.

Little Snow White was so hungry and thirsty that she ate

some vegetables and bread from each plate and drank a drop of wine out of each mug, for she did not wish to take all from one only. Then, as she was so tired, she laid herself down on one of the little beds, but none of them suited her; one was too long and another too short. At last she found that the seventh one was right, and so she remained in it, said a prayer, and went to sleep.

When it was quite dark the owners of the cottage came back. They were seven dwarfs who dug and delved in the mountains for ore. They lighted their seven candles, and as it was now light within the cottage they saw that someone had been there, for everything was not in the same order in which they had left it.

The first said, "Who has been sitting in my chair?"

"Who has been eating off my plate?" said the second.

"Who has been taking some of my bread?" said the third.

"Who has been eating my vegetables?" said the fourth.

"Who has been using my fork?" said the fifth.

"Who has been cutting with my knife?" said the sixth.

"Who has been drinking out of my mug?" said the seventh.

Then the first looked around and saw that there was a little dent in his sheets, and he said, "Who has been getting into my bed?" The others came up and each called out, "Somebody has been lying in my bed, too!" But the seventh, when he looked at his bed, saw little Snow White, who was lying asleep therein. He called the others, who came running up and cried out with astonishment, and brought their seven little candles and let the light fall on little Snow White.

"Oh, heavens! Oh, heavens!" cried they. "What a lovely child!" They were so glad that they did not wake her up, but let her sleep on in the bed. And the seventh dwarf slept with his companions, one hour with each, and so they got through the night.

When it was morning, little Snow White awoke and was frightened when she saw the seven dwarfs. But they were friendly and asked her what her name was. "My name is Snow White," she answered.

"How have you come to our house?" asked the dwarfs.

Then she told them that her stepmother had wished to have her killed, but that the huntsman had spared her life and that she had run for the whole day, until at last she had found their dwelling.

The dwarfs said, "If you will take care of our house, cook, make the beds, wash, sew, and knit, and if you will keep everything neat and clean, you can stay with us and you shall want for nothing."

"Yes," said Snow White, "with all my heart," and she stayed with them.

She kept the house in order for them. In the mornings they went to the mountains and looked for copper and gold; in the evenings they came back, and their supper had to be ready. The girl was alone the whole day, so the good dwarfs were careful to warn her.

"Beware of your stepmother; she will soon know that you are here. Be sure to let no one come in."

Meanwhile, the queen, believing that she had eaten Snow White's heart, could not but think that she was again the first and most beautiful of all. She went to her looking glass confidently and said,

> "Mirror, mirror, on the wall,
> Who in this land is the fairest of all?"

The glass answered—

> "Oh, Queen, you may possess a beauty quite rare,
> But over the hills, in the seven dwarfs' care,
> Dwells young Snow White and she is most fair
> For none with her beauty will ever compare."

Then the queen was astounded, for she knew that the looking glass never spoke falsely, which meant that the huntsman had betrayed her and that little Snow White was still alive.

And so the queen thought and thought again how she might kill her stepdaughter, for so long as she was not the fairest in the whole land, envy let her have no rest. When she had at last thought of something to do, she painted her face and dressed herself like an old peddler-woman, so no one could have known her.

In this disguise she went over the seven mountains to the house of the seven dwarfs, knocked at the door, and cried, "Pretty things to sell, very cheap, very cheap!" Little Snow White looked out of the window and called out, "Good day, my good woman, what have you to sell?"

"Good things, pretty things," she answered. "Laces of all colors." She pulled out one woven of brightly colored silk. *I will let the worthy old woman in*, thought Snow White, and she unbolted the door and bought the pretty laces.

"Child," said the old woman, "what a fright you look. Come, I will lace you properly for once." Snow White had no suspicion, but stood before her and let herself be laced with the new laces. But the old woman laced so quickly and so tightly that Snow White lost her breath and fell down as if dead. "Now I am once again the fairest in the land," said the queen to herself, and ran away.

Not long afterward, in the evening, the seven dwarfs came home. How shocked they were when they saw their dear little Snow White lying upon the ground! She neither stirred nor moved and seemed to be dead. They lifted her up and soon saw that she was laced too tightly. Miraculously, when they cut the laces, she began to breathe a little and after a while came to life again. When the dwarfs heard what had happened they said, "The old peddler-woman was no one else than the wicked queen; take care and let no one come in when we are not with you."

But the wicked woman when she had reached home went in front of the glass and asked,

> *"Mirror, mirror, on the wall,*
> *Who in this land is the fairest of all?"*

And it answered as before,

"Oh, Queen, you may possess a beauty quite rare,
But over the hills, in the seven dwarfs' care,
Dwells young Snow White and she is most fair
For none with her beauty will ever compare."

When she heard that, all her blood rushed to her heart with fear, for she saw plainly that little Snow White was again alive.

"But now," she said, "I will think of something that shall put an end to you." Then, by the help of witchcraft, which she understood, she made a poisonous comb and disguised herself in the shape of another old woman. Once again she went over the seven mountains to the seven dwarfs, knocked at the door, and cried, "Good things to sell, cheap, cheap!" Little Snow White looked out and said, "Go away! I cannot let anyone come in."

"I suppose you can look," said the old woman, and pulled the poisonous comb out and held it up. It pleased the girl so well that she let herself be beguiled, and opened the door. When they had made a bargain the old woman said, "Now I will comb you properly for once."

Poor little Snow White had no suspicion and let the old woman do as she pleased. But hardly had she put the comb in her hair than the poison in it took effect, and the girl fell down senseless. "You paragon of beauty," said the wicked woman, "you are done for now," and she went away.

But fortunately it was almost evening, when the seven dwarfs would come home. When they saw Snow White lying as if dead upon the ground they at once suspected the stepmother, and they looked and found the poisoned comb in the young girl's hair. Scarcely had they taken it out when Snow White came to, and told them what had happened. They warned her once more to be upon her guard and to open the door to no one.

The queen, back at the palace, went again in front of the glass and said,

> "Mirror, mirror, on the wall,
> Who in this land is the fairest of all?"

Then it answered as before,

> "Oh, Queen, you may possess a beauty quite rare,
> But over the hills, in the seven dwarfs' care,
> Dwells young Snow White and she is most fair
> For none with her beauty will ever compare."

When she heard the glass speak thus, she trembled and shook with rage. "Snow White shall die," she cried, "even if it costs me my life!"

Thereupon she went into a quite secret, lonely room, into which no one ever came, and there she made a very poisonous apple. Outside it looked pretty, white with a red cheek, so that everyone who saw it longed for it; but whoever ate a piece of it would surely die.

When the apple was ready she painted her face and dressed herself up as a country-woman, and she went over the seven mountains to the seven dwarfs.

Once again, she knocked at the door. Snow White put her head out of the window and said, "I cannot let anyone in; the seven dwarfs have forbidden me."

"It is all the same to me," answered the woman. "I shall soon get rid of my apples. There, I will give you one."

"No," said Snow White, "I dare not take anything."

"Are you afraid of poison?" said the old woman. "Look, I will cut the apple in two pieces; you eat the red cheek, and I will eat the white." The apple was so cunningly made that only the red cheek was poisoned.

Snow White longed for the fine apple, and when she saw that the woman ate part of it she could resist no longer. She stretched out her hand and took the poisonous half. But hardly had she a bit of it in her mouth than she fell down dead. Then the queen looked at her with a dreadful look, laughed aloud, and said, "White as snow, red as blood, black as ebony! This time the dwarfs cannot wake you up again."

And when she asked of her looking glass at home,

> *"Mirror, mirror, on the wall,*
> *Who in this land is the fairest of all?"*

It answered at last,

> *"Oh, Queen, in this land you are fairest of all."*

Then her envious heart had rest, so far as an envious heart can have rest.

The dwarfs, when they came home in the evening, found

Snow White lying upon the ground. She breathed no longer and was dead. They lifted her up, looked to see whether they could find anything poisonous, unlaced her, combed her hair, washed her with water and wine, but it was all of no use; the poor child was dead, and remained dead. They laid her upon a bier, and all seven of them sat around it and wept for her, and wept three days long.

Then they were going to bury her, but she still looked as if she were living and still had her pretty red cheeks. They said, "We could not bury her in the dark ground." Instead, they had a transparent coffin of glass made, so that she could be seen from all sides. They laid her in it and wrote her name, and that she was a king's daughter, upon it in golden letters. They put the coffin out upon the mountain, and one of them always stayed by it and watched it. And birds came, too, and wept for Snow White; first an owl, then a raven, and last a dove.

Snow White lay a long, long time in the coffin, and she did not change, but looked as if she were asleep. She was as white as snow, with lips as red as blood, and her hair was as black as ebony.

It happened, however, that a king's son came into the forest and went to the dwarfs' house to spend the night. He saw the coffin upon the mountain and the beautiful Snow White within it, and read what was written upon it in golden letters. Then he said to the dwarfs, "Let me have the coffin, I will give you whatever you want for it." But the dwarfs answered, "We will not part with it for all the gold in the world." Then he said, "Let me have it as a gift, for I cannot live without seeing Snow White. I will honor and prize her as my dearest possession." As he spoke in this way the good dwarfs took pity upon him and gave him the coffin.

Then, the king's son had the glass coffin carried away by his servants upon their shoulders, and it happened that they stumbled over a tree stump and shook Snow White's bier. With the jolt, the poisonous piece of apple which Snow White had bitten off came out of her throat. Before long, she opened her eyes, lifted up the lid of the coffin, sat up, and was once more alive. "Oh, heavens, where am I?" she cried. The king's son, full of joy, said, "You are with me." He told her what had happened, and said, "I love you more than everything in the world; come with me to my father's palace. You shall be my wife."

Snow White was willing, and went with him. Their wedding was held with great show and splendor. But Snow White's wicked stepmother was also bidden to the feast. When she had arrayed herself in beautiful clothes, she went before the looking glass, and said,

> "Mirror, mirror, on the wall,
> Who in this land is the fairest of all?"

The glass answered,

> "You are fairer than most, 'tis true
> But fairer still is the young queen than you."

Then the wicked woman uttered a curse and was so wretched, so utterly wretched, that she knew not what to do.

At first she would not go to the wedding at all, but she could have no peace until she saw the young queen. When she went in she knew Snow White; and she stood still with rage and fear, and could not stir.

Iron slippers had already been put upon the fire, and they were brought in with tongs and set before her. Then she was forced to put on the red-hot shoes and dance until she dropped down dead.

PUSS IN BOOTS

*

NCE upon a time, a miller died, leaving his mill to his eldest son, his donkey to his second son, and a cat to his youngest son.

The eldest son kept the mill, the second son took the donkey and set off in search of his fortune, but the third sat down upon a stone and sighed, "A cat! What am I going to do with that?"

But the cat heard his words and said, "Don't worry, Master. What do you think? That I'm worth less than a half-ruined mill or a mangy donkey? Give me a cloak, a hat with a feather in it, a bag, and a pair of boots, and you will see what I can do."

The young man, a bit surprised that his cat could speak, decided he had nothing to lose and gave the cat what he asked for. As he strode away, the cat said, "Do not look so glum, Master. I'll return soon!"

Swift of foot as he was, the cat soon caught a fat wild rabbit to put into his bag. Then he knocked at the castle gate, went before the king, and, removing his hat with a sweeping bow, he said:

"Sire, the famous Marquis of Carabas sends you this fine plump rabbit as a gift."

The king was very much amazed. But before he could speak, the cat had bowed and taken his leave.

The next day, the cat returned with some partridges tucked away in his bag. "Another gift from the brave Marquis of Carabas," he announced. The queen remarked, "This Marquis of Carabas is indeed a very courteous gentleman."

In the days that followed, the cat regularly visited the castle, carrying rabbits, hares, partridges, and skylarks, and presenting them all to the king in the name of the Marquis of Carabas. Soon, people at the palace began to discuss the Marquis.

"He must be a great hunter," someone remarked. "He must be very loyal to the king," said someone else. And yet another said, "But who is he? I've never heard of him." At this, someone who wanted to show people how much he knew replied, "Oh, yes, I've heard his name before. In fact, I knew his father."

The queen was very interested in this generous man who sent gifts to the king. "Is your master young and handsome?" she asked the cat.

"Oh, yes, and very rich, too," answered the feline. "In fact, he would be very honored if you and the king were to visit him in his castle." When the cat returned home and told his master that the king and queen were going to visit him, the miller's son was horrified.

"Whatever shall we do?" he cried. "As soon as they see me they will know how poor I am!"

"Leave everything to me," replied Puss in Boots. "I have a plan." For several days, the crafty cat kept on taking gifts to the king and queen, and one day he discovered that they were taking the princess on a carriage ride that very afternoon.

The cat hurried home in great excitement. "Master, come along!" he cried. "It is time to carry out my plan. You must go for a swim in the river."

"But I can't swim," replied the young man.

"That's all right," replied Puss in Boots. "Just trust me." So they went to the river, and when the king's carriage appeared the cat pushed his master into the water.

"Help!" cried the cat. "The Marquis of Carabas is drowning." The king heard his cries and sent his escorts to the rescue. They arrived just in time to save the poor man, who really was drowning. The king, the queen, and the princess fussed around and ordered new clothes to be brought for the Marquis of Carabas.

"Wouldn't you like to marry such a handsome man?" the queen asked the princess.

"Oh, yes," replied the princess. However, the cat overheard one of the ministers remark that they must find out how rich the marquis was.

"He is very rich indeed," said Puss in Boots. "He owns the castle and all this land. Come and see for yourself. I will meet you at the castle."

And with these words, the cat rushed off in the direction of the castle, shouting at the peasants working in the fields, "If anyone asks you who your master is, answer the Marquis of Carabas. If you don't, you will all be sorry." And so, when the king's carriage swept past, the peasants told the king that their master was the Marquis of Carabas.

In the meantime, Puss in Boots had arrived at the castle, the home of a huge, cruel ogre. Before knocking at the gate, the cat said to himself, "I must be very careful, or I'll never get out of here alive." When the door opened, Puss in Boots removed his feather hat and exclaimed, "My Lord Ogre, my respects!"

"What do you want, cat?" asked the ogre rudely.

"Sire, I've heard you possess great powers. That, for instance, you can change into a lion or an elephant."

"That's perfectly true," said the ogre.

"Well," said the cat, "I was talking to certain friends of mine who said that you would not be able to turn into a tiny little creature, like a mouse."

"Oh, so that's what they say, is it?" exclaimed the ogre.

The cat nodded and said, "Well, sire, that's my opinion, too. It seems impossible to me that you can turn yourself into not only an elephant, but also a wee mouse."

"Oh, yes? Well, just observe!" retorted the ogre, and turned into a mouse.

In a flash, the cat leapt upon the mouse and ate it whole. Then he dashed to the castle gate, just in time for the king's carriage was drawing up. With a bow, Puss in Boots said, "Sire, welcome to the castle of the Marquis of Carabas!" The king and queen, the princess, and the miller's son, who dressed in his princely clothes really did look like a marquis, got out of the carriage.

The king said, "My dear Marquis, you are a fine, handsome, young man, you have a great deal of land and a magnificent castle. Tell me, are you married?"

"No," the young man answered, "but I would like to find a

wife." He looked at the princess as he spoke. She, in turn, smiled at him.

The miller's son, now Marquis of Carabas, married the princess and lived happily with her in the castle. And from time to time, the cat would wink and whisper, "You see, Master, I am worth a lot more than any mangy donkey or half-ruined mill, am I not?"

THE ELVES
AND THE SHOEMAKER,
AND OTHER TALES

⚜

FIRST TALE

SHOEMAKER, by no fault of his own, had become so poor that at last he had nothing left but leather for one pair of shoes. So, in the evening, he cut out the shoes he wished to make the next morning, and, as he had a good conscience, he lay down quietly in his bed, commended himself to God, and fell asleep. In the morning, after he had said his prayers and was just going to sit down to work, he found the two shoes quite finished upon his table. He was astounded, and knew not what to say to it. He took the shoes in his hands to observe them closer, and they were so neatly made that there was not one bad stitch in them, just as if they were intended as a masterpiece.

Soon after, a buyer came in, and as the shoes pleased him so well, he paid more for them than was customary, and, with the money, the shoemaker was able to purchase leather for two pairs of shoes. He cut the shoes out at night and the next morning was about to set to work with fresh courage. But he had no need to do so, for when he got up they were already made. Once again, he found buyers, who gave him money enough to buy leather for four pairs of shoes.

The following morning, too, he found the four pairs made. And so it went on constantly, what he cut out in the evening was finished by the morning. He soon had his honest independence again, and at last became a wealthy man.

Now it befell that one evening not long before Christmas, when the man had been cutting out shoes, he said to his wife before going to bed, "What think you if we were to stay up tonight to see who it is that lends us this helping hand?" The woman liked the idea and lighted a candle, and then they hid themselves in a corner of the room behind some clothes which were hanging up there, and watched.

When it was midnight, two pretty little naked elves came, sat down by the shoemaker's table, took all the work which was cut out before them, and began to stitch, sew, and hammer so skillfully and so quickly with their little fingers that the shoemaker could not turn away his eyes for astonishment. They did not stop until all was done and stood finished upon the table, and then they ran quickly away.

The next morning the woman said, "The little men have made us rich, and we really must show that we are grateful for it. They run about so, and have nothing on, and must be cold. I'll tell you what I'll do: I will make them little shirts, coats, vests, and trousers, and knit both of them a pair of stockings, and do you, too, make them two little pairs of shoes." The man said, "I shall be very glad to do it."

At night, when everything was ready, instead of the usual cut-out leather, they laid their presents all together upon the table and then concealed themselves to see how the elves would behave. At midnight the elves came bounding in, and wanted to get to work at once, but as they did not find any leather cut out, only the pretty little articles of clothing, they were at first astonished, and then they showed intense delight. They dressed themselves with the greatest rapidity, putting the pretty clothes on, and singing,

> *"Now we are boys so fine to see,*
> *Why should we longer cobblers be?"*

Then they danced and skipped and leapt over chairs and benches. At last they danced out of doors. From that time forth they came no more, but as long as the shoemaker lived, all went well with him, and all his undertakings prospered.

SECOND TALE

THERE WAS ONCE a poor servant-girl, who was industrious and tidy, and swept the house every day and emptied her sweepings on a great heap outside of the door. One morning when she was just going back to her work, she found a letter upon this heap, and as she could not read, she put her broom in the corner and took the letter to her master and mistress. Behold, it was an invitation from the elves, who asked the girl to hold a child for them at its christening. The girl did not know what to do, but at length, after much persuasion, and as her master and mistress told her that it was not right to refuse an invitation of this kind, she consented.

Then three elves came and conducted her to a hollow mountain, where the little folks lived. Everything there was small, but more elegant and beautiful than can be described. The baby's mother lay in a bed of black ebony ornamented with pearls, the bedsheets were embroidered with gold; the cradle was of ivory, the bath of gold. After the girl stood as godmother, she wanted to go home again, but the little elves urgently entreated her to stay three days with them. So she stayed, and passed the time in pleasure and gaiety, and the little folks did all they could to make her happy.

At last when she was ready to set out upon her way home, the elves filled her pockets quite full of money, and after that they led her out of the mountain again. When she got home, she wanted to get back to her work and took the broom, which was still standing in the corner, in her hand and began to sweep. But then two strangers came out of the house and asked her who she was, and what business she had there? Alas, she had not, as she thought, been three days with the little men in the mountains, but seven years. In the meantime her former masters had died.

THIRD TALE

A CERTAIN MOTHER'S child had been taken away out of its cradle by the elves, and a changeling with a large head and staring eyes, which would do nothing but eat and drink, laid in its place. In her trouble the mother went to her neighbor and asked her advice. The neighbor advised her to carry the changeling into the kitchen, set it down upon the hearth, light a fire, and boil some water in two eggshells. This would make the changeling laugh, and if he laughed, he would lose his powers. The woman did everything that her neighbor bade her. When she put the eggshells with water on the fire, the imp said, "I am as old now as the Wester forest, but never yet have I seen anyone boil anything in an eggshell!"

And he began to laugh at it. While he was laughing, suddenly came a host of little elves, who brought the right child, set it down upon the hearth, and took the changeling away with them.

RUMPELSTILTSKIN

❋

NCE there was a miller who was poor, but who had a beautiful daughter. Now it happened that he had to go and speak to the king, and in order to make himself appear important he said to the king, "I have a daughter who can spin straw into gold."

The king said to the miller, "That is an art which pleases me well; if your daughter is as clever as you say, bring her tomorrow to my palace, and I will try what she can do."

When the girl was brought to him he took her into a room which was quite full of straw, gave her a spinning wheel and a reel, and said, "Now set to work, and if by tomorrow morning early you have not spun this straw into gold during the night, you must die." Thereupon he locked up the room and left her in it alone.

So there sat the poor miller's daughter, and for the life of her she could not tell what to do; she had no idea how straw could be spun into gold. She grew more and more miserable, until at last she began to weep.

All at once the door opened, and in came a little man, who said, "Good evening, Mistress Miller; why are you crying so?"

"Alas!" answered the girl. "I have to spin straw into gold, and I do not know how to do it."

"What will you give me," said the dwarf, "if I spin it for you?"

"My necklace," said the girl. The little man took the necklace, seated himself in front of the wheel, and *whirr, whirr, whirr,* in three turns the reel was full. Then he put another on, and *whirr, whirr, whirr,* three times around, and the second was full, too. And so it went on until the morning, when all the straw was spun and all the reels were full of gold. By daybreak the king was already there. When he saw the gold he was astonished and delighted, but his heart became only more greedy. He had the miller's daughter taken into another, much larger room full of straw, and commanded her to spin it all in one night if she valued her life. The girl knew not how to help herself, and was crying when the door again opened. The little man appeared and said, "What will you give me if I spin that straw into gold for you?"

"The ring on my finger," answered the girl.

The little man took the ring, again began to turn the wheel, and by morning had spun all the straw into glittering gold.

The king rejoiced beyond measure at the sight, but still he had not gold enough to satisfy his greed. He had the miller's daughter taken into a still larger room full of straw, and said, "You must spin this, too, in the course of this night; but if you succeed, you shall be my wife."

Even if she be a miller's daughter, thought he, *I could not find a richer wife in the whole world.*

When the girl was alone, the dwarf came again for the

third time, and said, "What will you give me if I spin the straw for you this time also?"

"I have nothing left that I could give," answered the girl.

"Then promise me, if you should become queen, your first child."

Who knows whether that will ever happen? thought the miller's daughter; and, not knowing how else to help herself in this strait, she promised the dwarf what he wanted, and for that, he once more spun the straw into gold.

When the king came in the morning and found all as he had wished, he took the girl in marriage, and the pretty miller's daughter became a queen.

After a year, she had a beautiful child, and she never gave a thought to the dwarf. But suddenly one day he came into her room, and said, "Now give me what you promised." The queen was horror-struck, and offered the dwarf all the riches of the kingdom if he would leave her the child. But the dwarf replied, "No, something that is living is dearer to me than all the treasures in the world." Then the queen began to weep and cry, so that the dwarf pitied her. "I will give you three days' time," said he. "If by that time you find out my name, then shall you keep your child."

So the queen thought the whole night of all the names that she had ever heard, and she sent a messenger over the country to inquire, far and wide, for any other names that there might be. When the dwarf came the next day, she began with Caspar, Melchior, Balthazar, and said all the names she knew, one after another; but to every one the little man said, "That is not my name." On the second day she had inquiries made in the neighborhood as to the names of the people there, and she repeated to the dwarf the most uncommon and curious. "Perhaps your name is Shortribs, or Sheepshanks, or Laceleg?" But he always answered, "That is not my name."

On the third day the messenger came back again and said, "I have not been able to find a single new name, but as I came to a high mountain at the end of the forest, where the fox and the hare bid each other good night, there I saw a little house. Before the house a fire was burning, and around the fire quite a ridiculous little man was jumping. He hopped upon one leg, and shouted,

> *"Today I bake, tomorrow brew,*
> *The next I'll have the young queen's child.*
> *Ha! Glad am I that no one knew*
> *That Rumpelstiltskin I am styled."*

You can imagine how glad the queen was when she heard the name! And when soon afterward the little man came in and asked, "Now, Mistress Queen, what is my name?" at first she said, "Is your name Conrad?"

"No."

"Is your name Harry?"

"No."

"Perhaps your name is Rumpelstiltskin?"

"The devil has told you that! The devil has told you that!" cried the little man. In his anger he plunged his right foot so deep into the earth that his whole leg went in; and then in rage he pulled at his left leg so hard with both hands that he tore himself in two.

THE WORN-OUT DANCING SHOES

HERE was once upon a time a king who had twelve daughters, each one more beautiful than the other. They all slept together in one chamber, in which their beds stood side by side, and every night when they were in them, the king locked the door, and bolted it. But in the morning when he unlocked the door, he saw that their shoes were worn out with dancing, and no one could find out how that had come to pass. Finally, the king proclaimed that whosoever could discover where his daughters danced at night should choose one of them for his wife and be king after his death, but that whosoever came forward and had not discovered it within three days and nights should have forfeited his life.

It was not long before a king's son presented himself and offered to undertake the enterprise. He was well received, and in the evening was led into a room adjoining the princesses' sleeping chamber. His bed was placed there, and he was to observe where they went and danced, and in order that they might do nothing secretly or go away to some other place, the door of their room was left open.

But the eyelids of the prince grew heavy as lead, and he soon fell asleep. When he awoke in the morning, all twelve daughters had been to the dance, for their shoes were standing there with holes in the soles. On the second and third nights it fell out just the same, and then his head was struck off without mercy. Many others came after this and undertook the enterprise, but all forfeited their lives.

Now it came to pass that a poor soldier, who had a wound and could serve no longer, found himself upon the road to the town where the king lived. There he met an old woman, who asked him where he was going.

"I hardly know myself," answered he, and added in jest, "I had half a mind to discover where the princesses danced their shoes into holes, and thus become king."

"That is not so difficult," said the old woman, "you must not drink the wine which will be brought to you at night, and must pretend to be sound asleep." With that she gave him a little cloak and said, "If you put that on, you will be invisible, and then you can steal after the twelve."

When the soldier had received this good advice, he approached the task in earnest, took heart, went to the king, and announced himself as a suitor. He was as well received as the others, and royal garments were put upon him. In the evening, he was lead into the antechamber, and as he was about to go to bed, the eldest daughter came and brought him a cup of wine. But he had tied a sponge under his chin, and let the wine run down into it, without drinking a drop. Then he lay down, and when he had lain a while, he began to snore as if in the deepest sleep. The twelve princesses heard that and laughed, and the eldest said, "He, too, might as well have saved his life."

With that they got up, opened wardrobes, presses, cupboards, and brought out pretty dresses. They dressed themselves before the mirrors, sprang about, and rejoiced at the prospect of the dance. Only the youngest said, "I know not how it is. You are very happy, but I feel very strange. Some misfortune is certainly about to befall us."

"You are a goose, who is always frightened," said the eldest. "Have you forgotten how many kings' sons have already come here in vain? I had hardly any need to give the soldier a sleeping draught, even without it the clown would not have awakened."

When they were all ready they looked carefully at the soldier, but he had closed his eyes and did not move or stir, so they felt themselves quite secure. The eldest then went to her bed and tapped it; it immediately sank into the earth, and one after the other they descended through the opening, the eldest going first. The soldier, who had watched everything, tarried no longer, put on his little cloak, and went down last with the youngest. Halfway down the steps, he trod just a little upon her dress. She was terrified at that, and cried out, "What is that? Who is pulling my dress?"

"Don't be so silly!" said the eldest. "You have caught it on a nail." Then they went all the way down, and when they were at the bottom, they were standing in a wonderfully pretty avenue of trees, all the leaves of which were silver, and shone and glistened. The soldier thought, *I must carry a token away with me,* and broke off a twig from one of them, upon which the tree cracked with a loud report. The youngest cried out again. "Something is wrong, did you hear the crack?" But the eldest said, "It is a joyful noise made by the princes we will soon set free."

After that they came into an avenue where all the leaves were of gold, and lastly into a third where they were of bright diamonds. The soldier broke off a twig from each, which made such a crack each time that the youngest started back in terror, but the eldest still maintained that they were salutes. They went on and came to a great lake whereon stood twelve little boats, and in every boat sat a handsome prince, all of whom were waiting for the twelve. Each took one of the princesses with him, but the soldier seated himself by the youngest. Then her prince said, "I can't tell why the boat is so much heavier today; I shall have to row with all my strength if I am to get it across."

"What should cause that," said the youngest, "but the warm weather? I feel very warm, too." On the opposite side of the lake stood a splendid, brightly-lighted castle, from whence resounded the joyous music of trumpets and kettle-drums. They rowed over to the castle, entered, and each prince danced with the girl he loved, and the soldier danced with them unseen. When one of the princesses had a cup of wine in her hand he drank it up, so that the cup was empty when she carried it to her mouth. The youngest was alarmed at this, but the eldest always made her be silent.

They danced there till three o'clock in the morning, when all the shoes were danced into holes, and they were forced to leave off. Then, the princes rowed them back again over the lake, and this time the invisible soldier seated himself by the eldest. On the shore the princesses took leave of their princes and promised to return the following night. When they reached the stairs the soldier ran on in front and lay down in his bed. When the twelve had come up slowly and wearily, he was already snoring so loudly that they could all hear him, and they said, "So far as he is concerned, we are safe." They took off their beautiful dresses, laid them away, put the worn-out shoes under the bed, and lay down.

The next morning the soldier was resolved not to speak, but to watch the wonderful goings on, and again went with them. Everything was done just as it had been done the first time, and each time they danced until their shoes were worn to pieces. But the third time he took a cup away with him as a token. When the hour had arrived for him to give his answer, he took the three twigs and the cup and went to the king. Meanwhile, the twelve stood behind the door and listened for what he was going to say.

When the king put the question, "Where have my twelve daughters danced their shoes to pieces in the night?" the soldier answered, "In an underground castle with twelve princes," and related how it had come to pass, and brought out the tokens. The king then summoned his daughters and asked them if the soldier had told the truth. When they saw that they were betrayed, and that falsehood would be of no avail, they were obliged to confess all. Thereupon the king asked which of them he would have to wife. He answered, "I am no longer young, so give me the eldest." The wedding was celebrated on the same day, and the kingdom was promised him after the king's death. But the princes were bewitched for as many days as they had danced nights with the twelve.

THE GOLDEN GOOSE

※

HERE was a man who had three sons, the youngest of whom was called Dummling and was despised, mocked, and put down on every occasion.

It happened that the eldest wanted to go into the forest to hew wood, and before he went his mother gave him a beautiful sweet cake and a bottle of wine in order that he might not suffer from hunger or thirst.

When he entered the forest there met him a little gray-haired old man who bade him good day, and said, "Do give me a piece of cake out of your pocket, and let me have a draught of your wine; I am so hungry and thirsty." But the prudent youth answered, "If I give you my cake and wine, I shall have none for myself. Be off with you." And he left the little man standing and went on.

But when he began to hew down a tree, it was not long before he made a false stroke, and the axe cut him in the arm so that he had to go home and have it bound up. And this was the little gray man's doing.

After this the second son went into the forest, and his mother gave him, like the eldest, a cake and a bottle of wine. The little old gray man met him likewise, and asked him for a piece of cake and a drink of wine. But the second son, too, said with much reason, "What I give you will be taken away from myself. Be off!" And he left the little man standing and went on. His punishment, however, was not delayed. When he had made a few strokes at the tree, he struck himself in the leg, so that he had to be carried home.

Then Dummling said, "Father, do let me go and cut wood."

The father answered, "Your brothers have hurt themselves with it. Leave it alone. You do not understand anything about it." But Dummling begged so long that at last he said, "Just go then, you will get wiser by hurting yourself." His mother gave him a cake made with water and baked in the cinders, and with it a bottle of sour beer.

When Dummling came to the forest the little old gray man met him likewise and, greeting him, said, "Give me a piece of your cake and a drink out of your bottle. I am so hungry and thirsty."

Dummling answered, "I have only cinder-cake and sour beer. If that pleases you, we will sit down and eat." So they sat down, and when Dummling pulled out his cinder-cake, it was a fine sweet cake, and the sour beer had become good wine. So they ate and drank, and afterward the little man said, "Since you have a good heart and are willing to divide what you have, I will give you good luck. There stands an old tree, cut it down, and you will find something at the roots." Then the little man took leave of him.

Dummling went and cut down the tree, and when it fell there was a goose with feathers of pure gold sitting in the roots. He lifted her up and, taking her with him, went to an inn where he thought he would stay the night. Now the host had three daughters, who saw the goose and were curious to know what such a wonderful bird might be, and would have liked to have one of its golden feathers.

The eldest thought, "I shall soon find an opportunity of pulling out a feather." As soon as Dummling had gone out she seized the goose by the wing, but her finger and hand remained stuck fast to it.

The second daughter came soon afterward, thinking only of how she might get a feather for herself, but she scarcely did she touch her sister than she was held fast to her.

At last the third also came with the like intent, and the others screamed out, "Keep away! For goodness' sake keep away!" But she did not understand why she was to keep away. *The others are there*, she thought, *I may as well be there, too.* She ran to them, but as soon as she had touched her sister, she remained sticking fast to her. So they all three had to spend the night with the goose.

The next morning, Dummling took the goose under his arm and set out, without troubling himself about the three girls who were hanging onto it. They were obliged to run after him continually, now left, now right, just as he was inclined to go.

In the middle of the fields the parson met them, and when he saw the procession he said, "For shame, you good-for-nothing girls! Why are you running across the fields after this young man? Is that seemly?" At the same time he seized the youngest by the hand in order to pull her away, but as soon as he touched her he likewise stuck fast and was himself obliged to run behind.

Before long the sexton came by and saw his master, the parson, running behind three girls. He was astonished at this and called out, "Your reverence, whither away so quickly? Do not forget that we have a christening today!" And running after him he took him by the sleeve, and was also held fast to it.

Whilst the five were trotting thus one behind the other, two laborers came with their hoes from the fields. The parson called out to them and begged that they would set him and the sexton free. But they had scarcely touched the sexton when they were held fast, and now there were seven of them running behind Dummling and the goose.

Soon afterward he came to a city, where a king ruled who had a daughter so serious that no one could make her laugh. The king, in desperation, had put forth a decree that whosoever should be able to make her laugh should marry her. When Dummling heard this, he went with his goose and all her train before the king's daughter, and as soon as she saw the seven people running on and on, one behind the other, she began to laugh quite loudly, as if she would never stop. Thereupon Dummling asked to have her for his wife, and the wedding was celebrated. After the king's death, Dummling inherited the kingdom and lived a long time contentedly with his wife.

OLD SULTAN

✤

FARMER once had a faithful dog called Sultan, who had grown old and lost all his teeth, so that he could no longer hold anything fast. One day the farmer was standing with his wife before their front door, and said, "Tomorrow I intend to shoot Old Sultan. He is no longer of any use to us."

His wife, who felt pity for the faithful beast, answered, "He has served us so long and been so faithful that we might well give him his keep."

"Eh! What?" said the man. "You are not very sharp. He has not a tooth left in his mouth, and no thief would be afraid of him. Now his time has come. If he has served us, he has had good feeding for it."

The poor dog, who was lying stretched out in the sun not far off, had heard everything, and was sorry that the morrow was to be his last day. He had a good friend, the wolf, and he crept out in the evening into the forest to him, and complained of the fate that awaited him.

"Hark ye, cousin," said the wolf, "be of good cheer. I will help you out of your trouble. I have thought of something. Tomorrow, early in the morning, your master is going with his wife to make hay, and they will take their little child with them since no one will be left behind in the house. They are wont, during work-time, to lay the child under the hedge in the shade. Lay yourself there, too, just as if you wished to guard it. Then I will come out of the wood, and carry off the child. You must rush swiftly after me, as if you would seize it again from me. I will let it fall, and you will take it back to its parents, who will think that you have saved it, and will be far too grateful to do you any harm. On the contrary, you will be in high favor, and they will never let you want for anything again."

The plan pleased the dog, and it was carried out just as it was arranged. The father screamed when he saw the wolf running across the field with his child, but when Old Sultan brought it back, he was full of joy, and stroked him and said, "Not a hair of yours shall be hurt, and you shall eat my bread free as long as you live." To his wife he said, "Go home at once and make Old Sultan some bread-sop that he will not have to bite, and bring the pillow out of my bed. I will give him that to lie upon."

Henceforth Old Sultan was as well off as he could wish to be.

Soon afterward the wolf visited him and was pleased that everything had succeeded so well. "But, cousin," said he, "you will just wink an eye if, when I have a chance, I carry off one of your master's fat sheep."

"Do not reckon upon that," answered the dog. "I will remain true to my master. I cannot agree to that."

The wolf, who thought that this could not be spoken in earnest, came creeping about in the night and was going to take away the sheep. But the farmer, to whom the faithful Sultan had told the wolf's plan, caught him and dressed his hide soundly with the flail. The wolf had to pack off, but he cried out to the dog, "Wait a bit, you scoundrel, you shall pay for this."

The next morning the wolf sent the boar to challenge the dog to come out into the forest so that they might settle the affair. Old Sultan could find no one to stand by him but a cat with only three legs. As they went out together the poor cat limped along, and at the same time stretched out her tail into the air with pain.

The wolf and his friend were already at the spot appointed, but when they saw their enemy coming, they thought that he was bringing a sabre with him, for they mistook the outstretched tail of the cat for one. And when the poor beast hopped on its three legs, they could only think every time that it was picking up a stone to throw at them. They were so afraid, the wild boar crept into the underwood and the wolf jumped up a tree.

The dog and the cat, when they came up, wondered that there was no one to be seen. The wild boar, however, had not been able to hide himself altogether, and one of his ears was still visible. While the cat was looking carefully about, the boar moved his ear. The cat, who thought it was a mouse moving, jumped upon it and bit it hard. The boar made a fearful noise and ran away, crying out, "The guilty one is up in the tree!" The dog and cat looked up and saw the wolf, who was ashamed of having shown himself so timid, and made his peace with the dog.

THE GOOSE-GIRL AT THE WELL

HERE was once upon a time a very old woman, who lived with her flock of geese in a lonely place amongst the mountains. Her little house was surrounded by a large forest, and every morning the old woman took her crutch and hobbled into the woods. The dame was quite active— more so than anyone would have thought considering her age. She collected grass for her geese, picked all the wild fruit she could reach, and carried everything home upon her back. Anyone would have thought that the heavy load would have weighed her to the ground, but she always brought it safely home.

If anyone met the old woman, she greeted him quite courteously. "Good day, dear countryman, it is a fine day. Ah! You wonder that I should drag grass about, but we must all take our burdens on our backs." Nevertheless, people did not like to meet her if they could help it, and took by preference a roundabout way. When a father with his boys passed her, he whispered to them, "Beware of the old woman. She has claws beneath her gloves; she is a witch."

One morning, a handsome young man was going through the forest. The sun shone bright, the birds sang, a cool breeze crept through the leaves, and he was full of joy and gladness. He had as yet seen no one when he suddenly perceived the old witch kneeling upon the ground cutting grass with a sickle. She had already thrust a whole load into her cloth, and near it stood two baskets, which were filled with wild apples and pears.

"But, good little mother," said he, "how can you carry all that away?"

"I must carry it, dear sir," answered she. "Rich folk's children have no need to do such things, but with the peasant folk the saying goes,

> *"Look forward, never back,*
> *Your spine curves like a sack."*

"Will you help me?" she said, as he remained standing by her. "You have still a straight back and young legs, it would be a trifle to you. Besides, my house is not so very far from here. It stands there upon the heath behind the hill. How soon you would bound up thither." The young man took compassion upon the old woman. "My father is certainly no peasant," replied he, "but a rich count. Nevertheless, that you may see that it is not only peasants who can carry things, I will take your bundle."

"If you will try it," said she, "I shall be very glad. You will certainly have to walk for an hour, but that shouldn't trouble you. You must carry those apples and pears as well." When he heard of an hour's walk, the young man began to have some doubts, but the old woman would not relent. Instead, she packed the bundle on his back, and hung the two baskets on his arm. "See, it is quite light," said she.

"No, it is not light," answered the count, and made a rueful face. "Verily, the bundle weighs as heavily as if it were full of cobblestones, and the apples and pears are as heavy as lead! I can scarcely breathe." He had a mind to put everything down again, but the old woman would not allow it.

"Just look," said she mockingly, "the young gentleman will not carry what I, an old woman, have so often dragged along. You are ready with fine words, but when it comes to action, you want to take to your heels. Why are you standing loitering there?" She continued, "Keep going. No one will take the bundle off again."

As long as the young man walked upon level ground, his load remained bearable, but when they came to the hill and had to climb, and the stones rolled down under his feet as if they were alive, it was beyond his strength. The drops of perspiration stood upon his forehead and ran, hot and cold, down his back.

"Dame," said he, "I can go no farther. I want to rest a little."

"Not here," answered the old woman, "when we have arrived at our journey's end, you can rest; but now you must go forward. Who knows what good it may do you?"

"Old woman, you are becoming shameless!" said the young count, and tried to throw off the bundle, but he labored in vain. His burden stuck as fast to his back as if it grew there. He turned and twisted, but he could not get rid of it. The old woman laughed at this and sprang about quite delighted upon her crutch.

"Don't get angry, dear sir," said she. "You are growing as red in the face as a rooster! Carry your bundle patiently. I will give you a good present when we get home."

What could he do? He was obliged to submit to his fate, and crawl along patiently behind the old woman. She seemed to grow more and more nimble, and his burden still heavier. All at once she made a spring, jumped onto the bundle and seated herself upon the top of it. However withered she might appear, she was yet heavier than the stoutest country lass. The youth's knees trembled, but when he did not go on, the old woman hit him about the legs with a switch and with stinging nettles.

Groaning continually, he climbed the mountain, and at length, when he was just about to drop, he reached the old woman's house. When the geese perceived the old woman, they flapped their wings, stretched out their necks, and ran to meet her, honking all the while. Behind the flock walked, stick in hand, an old wench, strong and big, but ugly as a toad.

"Good mother," said she to the old woman, "has anything happened to you, you have stayed away so long?"

"By no means, my dear daughter," answered she. "I have met with nothing bad, but, upon the contrary, with this kind gentleman, who has carried my burden for me. Only think, he even took me upon his back when I was tired. The way, too, has not seemed long to us. We have been merry, and have been cracking jokes with each other all the time."

At last the old woman slid down, took the bundle off the young man's back and the baskets from his arm, looked at him quite kindly, and said, "Now seat yourself upon the bench before the door, and rest. You have fairly earned your wages, and they shall not be wanting." Then she said to the goose-girl, "Go into the house, my dear daughter. It is not becoming for you to be alone with a young gentleman. One must not pour oil onto the fire, he might fall in love with you."

The count's son knew not whether to laugh or to cry. *Such a sweetheart as that,* thought he, *could not touch my heart, even if she were thirty years younger.*

In the meantime, the old woman stroked and petted her geese as if they were children, and then went into the house with her daughter. The youth lay down upon the bench under a wild apple tree. The air was warm and mild. On all sides stretched a green meadow set with cowslips, wild thyme, and a thousand other flowers. Through the midst of it rippled a clear brook upon which the sun sparkled, and the white geese went walking backward and forward or paddled in the water. "It is quite delightful here," said he, "but I am so tired that I cannot keep my eyes open. I will sleep a little. If only a gust of wind does not come and blow my legs off my body, for they are as weak as jelly."

When he had slept a little while, the old woman came and shook him till he awoke. "Sit up," said she. "You cannot not stay here; I have certainly treated you hardly, still it has not cost you your life. Of money and land you have no need, so here is something else for you." Thereupon she thrust a little box into his hand, which was cut out of a single emerald. "Take great care of it," said she. "It will bring you good fortune."

The count's son sprang up, and as he felt that he was quite fresh and had recovered his vigor, he thanked the old woman for her present and set off without even once looking back at the daughter. When he was already some way off, he still heard in the distance the noisy cry of the geese.

For three days the count's son had to wander in the wilderness before he could find his way out. He then reached a large town, and as no one knew him, he was led into the royal palace, where the king and queen were sitting on their thrones. The count's son fell upon one knee, drew the emerald box out of his pocket, and laid it at the queen's feet. She bade him rise and hand her the little box. Hardly had she opened it and looked therein, than she fell as if dead to the ground. The count's son was seized by the king's servants and was being led to prison, when the queen opened her eyes and ordered them to release him. Everyone was to go out, as she wished to speak with him in private.

When the queen was alone, she began to weep bitterly, and said, "Of what use to me are the splendors and honors with which I am surrounded! Every morning I awake in pain and sorrow. I had three daughters, the youngest of whom was so beautiful that the whole world looked upon her as a wonder. She was as white as snow, as rosy as apple blossom, and her hair as radiant as sunbeams. When she cried, tears did not fall from her eyes, but pearls and jewels only.

"When she was fifteen years old, the king summoned all

three sisters to come before his throne. You should have seen how all the people gazed when the youngest entered—it was just as if the sun were rising! Then the king spoke, 'My daughters, I know not when my last day may arrive. I will today decide what each of you shall receive at my death. You all love me, but the one of you who loves me best, shall fare the best.' Each of them said she loved him best.

"'Can you not express to me,' said the king, 'how much you do love me, and thus I shall see what you mean?'

"The eldest spoke. 'I love my father as dearly as the sweetest sugar.'

"The second, 'I love my father as dearly as my prettiest dress.'

"But the youngest was silent. Then the king said, 'And you, my dearest child, how much do you love me?'

"'I do not know, and can compare my love with nothing.'

"But her father insisted that she should name something. So she said at last, 'The best food does not please me without salt, therefore I love my father like salt.'

"When the king heard that, he fell into a passion and said, 'If you love me like salt, your love shall also be repaid with salt.' Then he divided the kingdom between the two elder daughters, but caused a sack of salt to be bound upon the back of the youngest, and two servants had to lead her forth into the wild forest. We all begged and prayed for her.

"But the king's anger was not to be appeased. How she cried when she had to leave us! The whole road was strewn with the pearls that flowed from her eyes.

"The king soon afterward repented his great severity, and

had the whole forest searched for the poor child, but no one could find her. When I think that the wild beasts have devoured her, I know not how to contain myself for sorrow. Many a time I console myself with the hope that she is still alive, and may have hidden herself in a cave or has found shelter with compassionate people. But picture to yourself, when I opened your little emerald box, a pearl lay therein, exactly the same kind as those which used to fall from my daughter's eyes. Then you can also imagine how the sight of it stirred my heart. You must tell me how you came by that pearl."

The count's son told her that he had received it from the old woman in the forest, who had appeared very strange to him and must be a witch, but he had neither seen nor heard anything of the queen's child. The king and the queen resolved to seek out the old woman. They thought that there where the pearl had been, they would obtain news of their daughter.

The old woman was sitting in that lonely place at her spinning wheel, spinning. It was already dusk, and a log which was burning upon the hearth gave a scanty light. All at once, there was a noise outside. The geese were coming home from the pasture, uttering their hoarse cries. Soon afterward the daughter also entered. But the old woman scarcely thanked her and only shook her head a little. The daughter sat down beside her, took her spinning wheel, and twisted the threads as nimbly as a very young girl.

Thus they both sat for two hours and exchanged never a

word. At last something rustled at the window, and two fiery eyes peered in. It was an old night owl, which cried, "Hoo-hoo!" three times. The old woman looked up just a little, then said, "Now, my little daughter, it is time for you to go out and do your work."

The daughter rose and went out, and where did she go? Over the meadows ever onward into the valley. At last she came to a well with three old oak trees standing beside it. Meanwhile, the moon had risen large and round over the mountain, and it was so light that one could have found a needle. She removed the skin which covered her face, then bent down to the well and began to wash herself. When she had finished, she dipped the skin also in the water and then laid it down on the meadow, so that it should bleach in the moonlight and dry again.

But how the maiden was changed! Such a change as that was never seen before! When the gray mask fell off, her golden hair broke forth like sunbeams and spread about like a mantle over her whole form. Her eyes shone out as brightly as the stars in heaven, and her cheeks bloomed a soft red like apple blossom.

But the fair maiden was sad. She sat down and wept bitterly. One pearl tear after another forced itself out of her eyes and rolled through her long hair to the ground. There she sat, and would have remained sitting a long time, if there had not been a rustling and cracking in the boughs of the neighboring tree. At the sound, she sprang up like a doe which has been overtaken by the shot of the hunter. Just then the moon was obscured by a dark cloud, and in an instant the maiden had put on the old skin and vanished, like a light blown out by the wind.

She ran back home, trembling like an aspen leaf. The old woman was standing upon the threshold. The girl was about to relate what had befallen her, but the old woman laughed kindly and said, "I already know all." She led her into the room and lighted a new log. She did not, however, sit down to her spinning again, but fetched a broom and began to sweep and scour. "All must be clean and sweet," she said to the girl.

"But, Mother," said the maiden, "why do you begin work at so late an hour? What do you expect?"

"Do you know then what time it is?" asked the old woman.

"Not yet midnight," answered the maiden, "but already past eleven o'clock."

"Do you not remember," continued the old woman, "that it is three years today since you came to me? Your time is up, we can no longer remain together."

The girl was terrified, and said, "Alas! Dear Mother, will you cast me off? Where shall I go? I have no friends, and no home to which I can go. I have always done as you bade me, and you have always been satisfied with me. Do not send me away."

The old woman would not tell the maiden what lay before her. "My stay here is over," she said to her, "but when I depart, the house and parlor must be clean. Therefore, do not hinder me in my work. Have no care for yourself, you shall find a roof to shelter you, and the wages which I will give you shall also content you."

"But tell me what is about to happen," the maiden continued to entreat.

"I tell you again, do not hinder me in my work. Do not say a word more, go to your chamber, take the skin off your face, and put on the silken gown which you had on when you came to me, and then wait in your chamber until I call you."

But I must once more tell of the king and queen, who had journeyed forth with the count's son in order to seek out the old woman in the wilderness. The count's son had strayed away from them in the wood by night, and had to walk onward alone. The next day it seemed to him that he was upon the right track. He still went forward until darkness came on, then he climbed a tree, intending to pass the night there, for he feared that he might lose his way.

When the moon illuminated the surrounding country, he perceived a figure coming down the mountain. She had no stick in her hand, but yet he could see that it was the goose-girl, whom he had seen before in the house of the old woman.

"Oh-ho!" cried he. "There she comes, and if I once get hold of one of the witches, the other shall not escape me!"

But how astonished he was when she went to the well, took off the skin, and washed herself. When her golden hair fell down all about her, she was more beautiful than anyone whom he had ever seen in the whole world. He hardly dared to breathe, but stretched his head as far forward through the leaves as he dared, and stared at her.

Either he bent over too far or whatever the cause might be, the bough suddenly cracked, and that very moment the maiden slipped into the skin, sprang away like a doe, and, as the moon was suddenly covered, disappeared from his eyes. Hardly had she disappeared before the count's son descended from the tree and hastened after her with nimble steps. He had not been gone long before he saw, in the twilight, two figures coming over the meadow. It was the king and queen, who had perceived from a distance the light shining in the old woman's little house and were going to it. The count's son told them what wonderful things he had seen by the well, and they did not doubt that it had been their lost daughter.

They walked onward full of joy, and soon came to the little house. The geese were sitting all around it and had thrust their heads under their wings and were sleeping, and not one of them moved. The king and queen looked in at the window, the old woman was sitting there quite quietly spinning, nodding her head and never looking around. The room was perfectly clean, as if the little mist men, who carry no dust on their feet, lived there. Their daughter, however, they did not see. They gazed at all this for a long time, at last they took heart, and knocked softly at the window. The old woman appeared to have been expecting them. She rose, and called out quite kindly, "Come in, I know you already."

When they had entered the room, the old woman said, "You might have spared yourself the long walk, if you had not three years ago unjustly driven away your child, who is so good and lovable. No harm has come to her. For three years she has had to tend the geese. With them she has learned no evil, but has preserved her purity of heart. You, however, have been sufficiently punished by the misery in which you have lived."

Then she went to the chamber and called, "Come out, my little daughter." Thereupon the door opened, and the princess stepped out in her silken garments, with her golden hair and her shining eyes. It was as if an angel from heaven had entered.

She went up to her father and mother, fell upon their necks, and kissed them. There was no help for it, they all had to weep for joy. The young count's son stood near them, and when she perceived him she became as red in the face as a rose. She herself did not know why. The king said, "My dear child, I have given away my kingdom, what shall I give you?"

"She needs nothing," said the old woman. "I give her the tears that she has wept on your account. They are precious pearls, finer than those that are found in the sea, and worth more than your whole kingdom. And I give her my little house as payment for her services." When the old woman had said that, she disappeared from their sight. The walls rattled a little, and when the king and queen looked around, the little house had changed into a splendid palace, a royal table had been spread, and the servants were running hither and thither.

The story goes still further, but my grandmother, who related it to me, had partly lost her memory and had forgotten the rest. I shall always believe that the beautiful princess married the count's son and that they remained together in the palace, and lived there in all happiness so long as God willed it.

Whether the snow-white geese, which were kept near the little hut, were verily young maidens whom the old woman had taken under her protection, and whether they now received their human form again and stayed as handmaids to the young queen, I do not exactly know, but I suspect it.

This much is certain, that the old woman was no witch, as people thought, but a wise woman who meant well. Very likely it was she who, at the princess's birth, gave her the gift of weeping pearls instead of tears. That does not happen nowadays, or else the poor would soon become rich.

KING THRUSHBEARD

✣

KING had a daughter who was beautiful beyond all measure, but was so proud and haughty that no suitor was good enough for her. She sent away one after the other and ridiculed them as well.

Once the king made a great feast and all the young men likely to marry from far and near were invited to attend. They were all marshaled in a row according to their rank and standing. First came the kings, then the grand dukes, then the princes, the earls, the barons, and the gentry. Then the king's daughter was led through the ranks, but to every one she had some objection to make. One was too fat: "That barrel," she said. Another was too tall: "Long and thin has little in." The third was too short: "Short and thick is never quick." The fourth was too pale: "As pale as death." The fifth too red: "A fighting cock." The sixth was not straight enough: "A green log dried behind the stove."

She had something to say against every one, but she made herself especially merry over a good king who stood quite high up in the row, whose chin had grown a little crooked. "Well," she cried and laughed, "he has a chin like a thrush's beak!" And from that time he got the name of King Thrush-beard.

But the old king, when he saw that his daugher did nothing but mock the people and despised all the suitors who were gathered there, was very angry, and swore that she should have for her husband the very first beggar who came to his doors.

A few days afterward a fiddler came and sang beneath the windows, trying to earn a small alms. When the king heard him he said, "Let him come up." So the fiddler came in, in his dirty, ragged clothes, and sang before the king and his daughter. When he had ended he asked for a trifling gift. The king said, "Your song has pleased me so well that I will give you my daughter there for your wife."

The king's daughter shuddered, but the king said, "I have taken an oath to give you to the very first beggar-man, and I will keep it." All she could say was in vain; the priest was brought, and she had to let herself be wedded to the fiddler that very afternoon. When that was done the king said, "Now it is not proper for you, a beggar-woman, to stay any longer in my palace. You may just go away with your husband."

The beggar-man led her out by the hand, and she was obliged to walk away on foot with him. When they came to a large forest she asked, "To whom does that beautiful forest belong?"

"It belongs to King Thrushbeard; if you had taken him, it would have been yours."

"Ah, unhappy girl that I am, if I had but taken King Thrushbeard!"

Afterward they came to a meadow, and she asked again, "To whom does this beautiful green meadow belong?"

"It belongs to King Thrushbeard; if you had taken him, it would have been yours."

"Ah, unhappy girl that I am, if I had but taken King Thrushbeard!"

Then they came to a large town, and she asked again, "To whom does this fine large town belong?"

"It belongs to King Thrushbeard; if you had taken him, it would have been yours."

"Ah, unhappy girl that I am, if I had but taken King Thrushbeard!"

"It does not please me," said the fiddler, "to hear you always wishing for another husband. Am I not good enough for you?" At last they came to a little hut, and she said, "Oh, goodness! What a small house! To whom does this miserable, mean hovel belong?" The fiddler answered, "That is my house and yours, where we shall live together."

She had to stoop in order to go in at the low door. "Where are the servants?" said the king's daughter.

"What servants?" answered the beggar-man. "You must do what you wish to have done. Just make a fire at once, and prepare water to cook my supper. I am quite tired." But the king's daughter knew nothing about lighting fires or cooking, and the beggar-man had to lend a hand himself to get anything fairly done. When they had finished their scanty meal they went to bed; but he forced her to get up quite early in the morning in order to look after the house.

For a few days they lived in this way as well as might be,

but they soon came to the end of all their provisions. The man said, "Wife, we cannot go on any longer eating and drinking here and earning nothing. You must weave baskets." He went out, cut some willows, and brought them home. Then she began to weave, but the tough willows wounded her delicate hands.

"I see that this will not do," said the man. "You had better spin. Perhaps you can do that better." She sat down and tried to spin, but the hard thread soon cut her soft fingers so that the blood ran down. "See," said the man, "you are fit for no sort of work; I have made a bad bargain with you. Now I will try to make a business with pots and earthenware; you must sit in the marketplace and sell the wares."

Alas, thought she, *if any of the people from my father's kingdom come to the market and see me sitting there, selling, how they will mock me.* But it was of no use, she had to yield unless she chose to die of hunger.

For the first time she succeeded well, for the people were glad to buy the woman's wares because she was good-looking, and they paid her what she asked. Many even gave her the money and left the pots with her as well. So they lived on what she had earned as long as it lasted, then the husband bought a lot of new crockery. With this she sat down at the corner of the marketplace and set it out around her ready for sale. But suddenly there came a drunken hussar galloping along, and he rode right amongst the pots so that they were all broken into a thousand bits. She began to weep and did now know what to do for fear. "Alas! What will happen to me?" cried she. "What will my husband say to this?"

She ran home and told him of the misfortune. "Who would seat herself at a corner of the marketplace with crockery?" said the man. "Leave off crying. I see very well that you cannot do any ordinary work, so I have been to our king's palace and have asked whether they cannot find a place for a kitchen maid, and they have promised me to take you. In that way you will get your food for nothing."

The king's daughter was now a kitchen maid, and had to be at the cook's beck and call, and do the dirtiest work. In both her pockets she fastened little jars, in which she took home her share of the leavings, and upon this they lived.

It happened that the wedding of the king's eldest son was to be celebrated, so the poor woman went up and placed herself by the door of the hall to look on. When all the candles were lit, and people, each more beautiful than the other, entered, and all was full of pomp and splendor, she thought of her lot with a sad heart. She cursed the pride and haughtiness which had humbled her and brought her to so great poverty.

The smell of the delicious dishes which were being taken in and out reached her, and now and then the servants threw her a few morsels of them. These she put in her jars to take home.

All at once the king's son entered, clothed in velvet and silk, with gold chains about his neck. When he saw the beautiful woman standing by the door he seized her by the hand, and would have danced with her. But she refused and shrank with fear, for she saw that it was King Thrushbeard, her suitor whom she had driven away with scorn. Her struggles were of no avail, and he drew her into the hall; but the string by which her pockets were hung snapped, the pots fell down, the soup ran out, and the scraps were scattered all about. When the people saw it, there arose general laughter and derision, and she was so ashamed that she would rather have been a thousand fathoms below the ground.

She sprang to the door and would have run away, but on the stairs a man caught her and brought her back. When she looked at him it was King Thrushbeard again. He said to her kindly, "Do not be afraid, I and the fiddler who has been living with you in that wretched hovel are one. For love of you I disguised myself so; and I also was the hussar who rode through your crockery. This was all done to humble your proud spirit, and to punish you for the insolence with which you mocked me."

Then she wept bitterly and said, "I have done great wrong, and am not worthy to be your wife." But he said, "Be comforted, the evil days are past; now we will celebrate our wedding." Then the maids-in-waiting came and dressed her in the most splendid clothing. Her father and his whole court came and wished her happiness in her marriage with King Thrushbeard, and the joy now began in earnest.

SWEETHEART ROLAND

✣

HERE was once upon a time a woman who was a real witch and had two daughters. One was ugly and wicked, and this one she loved because she was her own daughter. And one was beautiful and good, and this one she hated because she was her stepdaughter. The stepdaughter once had a pretty apron, which the other fancied so much that she became envious and told her mother that she must and would have it.

"Be quiet, my child," said the old woman, "and you shall have it. Your stepsister has long deserved to die. Tonight when she is asleep I will come and cut her head off. Only be careful that you are at the far side of the bed, and push her well to the front."

It would have been all over with the stepdaughter if she had not just then been standing in a corner, and heard everything. All day long she dared not go out of doors. Then, when bedtime came, the witch's daughter got into bed first, so as to lie at the far side. But when she was asleep, the other pushed her gently to the front and took for herself the place at the back, close by the wall. In the night, the old woman came creeping in with an axe in her right hand, and felt with her left to see if anyone was lying at the outside. Then she grasped the axe with both hands and cut her own child's head off.

When she had gone away, the girl got up and went to her sweetheart, who was called Roland, and knocked at his door. When he came out, she said to him, "Hear me, dearest Roland, we must fly in all haste. My stepmother wanted to kill me, but has struck her own child. When daylight comes and she sees what she has done, we shall be lost."

"But," said Roland, "I counsel you first to take away her magic wand, or we cannot escape if she pursues us." The maiden fetched the magic wand, and she took the dead girl's head and dropped three drops of blood upon the ground, one in front of the bed, one in the kitchen, and one upon the stairs. Then she hurried away with her lover.

When the old witch got up next morning, she called her daughter and wanted to give her the apron, but she did not come. Then the witch cried, "Where are you?"

"Here, upon the stairs, I am sweeping," answered the first drop of blood. The old woman went out, but saw no one upon the stairs, and cried again, "Where are you?"

"Here in the kitchen, I am warming myself," cried the second drop of blood. The witch went into the kitchen, but found no one. Then she cried again, "Where are you?"

"Ah, here in the bed, I am sleeping," cried the third drop of blood. She went into the room to the bed. What did she see there? Her own child, whose head she had cut off, bathed in her blood. The witch, in a rage, sprang to the window, and as she could look forth quite far into the world, she perceived her stepdaughter hurrying away with her sweetheart Roland.

"That shall not serve you!" cried she. "Even if you have got a long way off, you shall still not escape me." She put on her many-league boots, in which she went an hour's walk at every step, and it was not long before she overtook them.

The girl, when she saw the old woman striding toward her, used the magic wand to change her sweetheart Roland into a lake and herself into a duck swimming in the middle of it. The witch placed herself on the shore, threw breadcrumbs in, and gave herself every possible trouble to entice the duck. But the duck did not let herself be enticed, and the old woman had to go home at night as she had come.

On this the girl and her sweetheart Roland resumed their natural shapes again, and they walked on the whole night until daybreak. Then the maiden changed herself into a beautiful flower which stood in the midst of a briar hedge, and her sweetheart Roland into a fiddler. It was not long before the witch came striding up toward them, and said to the musician, "Dear musician, may I pluck that beautiful flower for myself?"

"Oh, yes," he replied. "I will play to you while you do it."

As she was hastily creeping into the hedge and was just going to pluck the flower, for she well knew who the flower was, he began to play. Whether she wanted to or not, she was forced to dance, for it was a magical tune. The quicker he played, the more violent springs was she forced to make, and the thorns tore her clothes from her body, and pricked her and wounded her till she bled. As he did not stop, she had to dance till she lay dead upon the ground.

When they were safe, Roland said, "Now I will go to my father and arrange for the wedding."

"Then in the meantime I will stay here and wait for you," said the girl, "and that no one may recognize me, I will change myself into a red stone landmark."

Then Roland went away, and the girl changed into a red landmark in the field and waited for her beloved. But when Roland got home, he fell into the snares of another woman, who prevailed upon him so far that he forgot the maiden. The poor girl remained there a long time. But at length, as he did not return at all, she was sad and changed herself into a flower, and thought, *Someone will surely come this way and trample me down.*

It befell, however, that a shepherd kept his sheep in the field and saw the flower. As it was so pretty, he plucked it, took it with him, and laid it away in his chest. From that time forth, strange things happened in the shepherd's house. When he arose in the morning, all the work was already done, the room was swept, the table and benches cleaned, the fire upon the hearth was lighted, and the water was fetched. At noon, when he came home, the table was laid and a good dinner served.

He could not conceive how this came to pass, for he never saw a human being in his house, and no one could have concealed herself in it. He was certainly pleased with this good attendance, but at last he was so perplexed that he went to a wise woman and asked for her advice. The wise woman said, "There is some enchantment behind it, listen very early some morning if anything is moving in the room, and if you see anything, let it be what it may, throw a white cloth over it, and then the magic will be stopped."

The shepherd did as she bade him, and the next morning just as day dawned, he saw the chest open, and the flower come out. Swiftly he sprang toward it and threw a white cloth over it. Instantly the transformation came to an end, and a beautiful girl stood before him. She owned to him that she had been the flower, and that up to this time she had attended to his housekeeping. She told him her story, and as she pleased him he asked her if she would marry him, but she answered, "No," for she wanted to remain faithful to her sweetheart Roland, although he had deserted her. Still, she promised not to go away, but to keep house for the shepherd for the future.

Now the time drew near when Roland's wedding was to be celebrated. According to an old custom in the country, it was announced that all the girls were to be present at it, and sing in honor of the bridal pair. When the faithful maiden heard of this, she grew so sad that she thought her heart would break, and she would not have gone thither, if the other girls hadn't come and taken her. When it came time to sing, she stepped back until at last she was the only one left, and then she could not refuse. But when she began her song, and it reached Roland's ears, he sprang up and cried, "I know the voice, that is my true bride! I will have no other!" Everything he had forgotten, and which had vanished from his mind, had suddenly come home again to his heart. Then the faithful maiden held her wedding with her sweetheart Roland, and grief came to an end and joy began.

THE TWO BROTHERS

⚜

HERE were once upon a time two brothers, one rich and the other poor. The rich one was a goldsmith and evil-hearted. The poor one supported himself by making brooms, and was good and honorable. The poor one had two children, who were twin brothers and as like each other as two drops of water. Once in a while, the two boys were allowed to go to their rich uncle's house and get some of the scraps to eat.

One day, when the poor man was going into the forest to fetch brushwood, he saw a bird which was quite golden and more beautiful than any he had ever chanced to meet with. He picked up a small stone, threw it at him, and was lucky enough to hit him, but only one golden feather fell down, and the bird flew away. The man took the feather and carried it to his brother, who looked at it and said, "It is pure gold!" and gave him a great deal of money for it.

The next day the man climbed into a birch tree, and was about to cut off a couple of branches when the same bird flew out. When the man searched he found a nest, and inside it lay an egg of gold. He took the egg home with him and carried it to his brother, who again said, "It is pure gold," and gave him what it was worth.

At last the goldsmith said, "I should indeed like to have the bird itself." The poor man went into the forest for the third time, and again saw the golden bird sitting on the tree, so he took a stone, knocked it down, and carried it to his brother, who gave him a great heap of gold for it. *Now I can provide for my sons,* thought he, and went contentedly home.

The goldsmith was crafty and cunning, and knew very well what kind of a bird it was. He called his wife and said, "Roast me the gold bird, and take care that none of it is lost. I have a fancy to eat it all myself."

The bird was no common one, but of so wondrous a kind that whosoever ate its heart and liver found every morning a piece of gold beneath his pillow.

The woman made the bird ready, put it upon the spit, and let it roast. Now it happened that while it was at the fire, and the woman was forced to go out of the kitchen on account of some other work, the two children of the poor broom maker ran in, stood by the spit, and turned it around once or twice.

At that very moment two little bits of the bird fell down into the dripping tin, one of the boys said, "Let us eat these two little bits. I am so hungry, and no one will ever miss them."

Then the two ate the pieces. Just then the woman came into the kitchen, saw that they were eating something, and said, "What have you been eating?"

"Two little morsels which fell out of the bird," answered they.

"That must have been the heart and the liver," said the woman, quite frightened. In order that her husband might not miss them and be angry, she quickly killed a young cock, took out his heart and liver, and put them beside the golden bird. When it was ready, she carried it to the goldsmith, who consumed it all alone and left none of it.

The next morning, however, when he felt beneath his pillow and expected to bring out the piece of gold, no more gold pieces were there than there had always been.

The two children did not know what a piece of good fortune had fallen to their lot.

The next morning when they arose, something fell rattling to the ground, and when they picked it up there were two gold pieces! They took them to their father, who was astonished and said, "How can that have happened?"

When the next morning they again found two, and so on daily, he went to his brother and told him the strange story. The goldsmith at once knew how it had come to pass and that the children had eaten the heart and liver of the golden bird. In order to revenge himself, and because he was envious and hard-hearted, he said to the father, "Your children are in league with the Evil One. Do not take the gold, and do not suffer them to stay any longer in your house, for he has them in his power, and may ruin you likewise."

The father feared the Evil One, and painful as it was to him, he nevertheless led the twins forth into the forest and with a sad heart left them there. The two children ran about the forest and sought the way home again, but could not find it, and only lost themselves more and more. At length they met with a huntsman, who asked, "To whom do you children belong?"

"We are the poor broom maker's boys," they replied, and they told him that their father would not keep them any longer in the house because a piece of gold lay every morning under their pillows.

"Come," said the huntsman, "that is nothing so very bad, if at the same time you keep honest and are not idle."

As the good man liked the children and had none of his own, he took them home with him and said, "I will be your father, and bring you up till you are big." They learned huntsmanship from him, and the piece of gold which each of them found when he awoke was kept for them by the huntsman in case they should need it in the future.

When they were grown up, their foster father one day took them into the forest with him and said, "Today shall you make your trial shot, so that I may release you from your apprenticeship and make you huntsmen."

They went with him to lie in wait and stayed there a long time, but no game appeared. The huntsman, however, looked above him and saw a covey of wild geese flying in the form of a triangle, and said to one of them, "Shoot me down one from each corner." He did it, and thus accomplished his trial shot.

Soon after another covey came flying by in the form of the figure two, and the huntsman bade the other also bring down one from each corner, and his trial shot was likewise successful.

"Now," said the foster father, "I pronounce you out of your apprenticeships. You are skilled huntsmen."

Thereupon the two brothers went forth together into the forest, took counsel with each other, and formed a plan. In the evening when they had sat down to supper, they said to their foster father, "We will not touch food, or take one mouthful, until you have granted us a request."

Said he, "What, then, is your request?"

They replied, "We have now finished learning, and we must prove ourselves in the world, so allow us to go away and travel."

Then spoke the old man joyfully, "You talk like brave huntsmen. That which you desire has been my wish. Go forth. All will go well with you." Thereupon they ate and drank joyously together.

When the appointed day came, their foster father presented each of them with a good gun and a dog, and let each of them take as many of his saved-up gold pieces as he chose. Then he accompanied them a part of the way, and when taking leave, he gave them a bright knife and said, "If ever you separate, stick this knife into a tree at the place where you part. When one of you goes back, he will be able to see how his absent brother is faring, for the side of the knife which is turned in the direction by which he went will rust if he dies, but will remain bright as long as he is alive."

The two brothers went still farther onward, and came to a forest which was so large that it was impossible for them to get out of it in one day. So they passed the night in it and ate what they had put in their hunting pouches. They walked all the second day likewise, and still did not get out.

As they had nothing to eat, one of them said, "We must shoot something for ourselves or we shall suffer from hunger." Then he loaded his gun, and looked about him.

When an old hare came running up toward them, he laid his gun upon his shoulder, but the hare cried,

> *"Dear huntsman, do but let me live,*
> *Two little ones to you I'll give,"*

and sprang instantly into the thicket and brought two young ones. The little creatures played so merrily, and were so pretty, that the huntsmen could not find it in their hearts to kill them. They, therefore, kept them with them, and the little hares followed on foot. Soon after this, a fox crept past. They were just going to shoot it, but the fox cried,

> *"Dear hunstman, do but let me live,*
> *Two little ones I'll also give!"*

He, too, brought two little foxes, and the huntsmen did not like to kill them either, but gave them to the hares for company, and they followed behind. It was not long before a wolf strode out of the thicket. The huntsmen made ready to shoot him, but the wolf cried,

> *"Dear huntsman, do but let me live,*
> *Two little ones I'll likewise give!"*

The huntsmen put the two wolves beside the other animals, and they followed behind them. Then a bear came who wanted to trot about a little longer, and cried:

"Dear huntsman, do but let me live,
Two little ones I, too, will give."

The two young bears were added to the others, and there were already eight of them. At length who came? A lion came, and tossed his mane. But the huntsmen did not let themselves be frightened and aimed at him likewise, and the lion also said,

"Dear huntsman, do but let me live,
Two little ones I, too, will give."

And he brought his little ones to them, and now the huntsmen had two lions, two bears, two wolves, two foxes, and two hares, who followed them and served them. In the meantime their hunger was not appeased by this, and they said to the foxes, "Hark, cunning fellows, provide us with something to eat. You are crafty and deep."

They replied, "Not far from here lies a village from which we have already brought many a fowl. We will show you the way there."

So they went into the village, bought themselves something to eat, had some food given to their beasts, and then traveled onward. The foxes knew their way very well about the district and where the poultry yards were, and were able to guide the huntsmen.

Now they traveled about for a while, but could find no situations where they could remain together, so they said, "There is nothing else for it, we must part." They divided the animals so that each of them had a lion, a bear, a wolf, a fox, and a hare. Then they took leave of each other, promised to love each other like brothers till their death, and stuck the knife which their foster father had given them into a tree, after which one went east and the other went west.

The younger arrived with his beasts in a town which was all hung with black crepe. He went into an inn and asked the host to accommodate his animals. The innkeeper gave him a stable where there was a hole in the wall. The hare crept out and fetched himself the head of a cabbage, and the fox fetched himself a hen and, when he had devoured that, got the cock as well. But the wolf, the bear, and the lion could not get out because they were too big. Then the innkeeper let them be taken to a place where a cow was grazing, so that they might eat till they were satisfied.

When the huntsman had taken care of his animals, he asked the innkeeper why the town was thus hung with black crepe. Said the host, "Because our king's only daughter is to die tomorrow."

The huntsman inquired if she was sick unto death.

"No," answered the host, "she is vigorous and healthy, nevertheless she must die!"

"How is that?" asked the huntsman.

"There is a high hill outside the town, where dwells a dragon who every year must have a pure maiden or he lays the whole country waste. All the maidens have already been given to him, and there is no longer anyone left but the king's daughter, yet there is no mercy for her. She must be given up to him, and that is to be done tomorrow."

Said the huntsman, "Why is the dragon not killed?"

"Ah," replied the host, "so many knights have tried it, but it has cost all of them their lives. The king has promised that he who conquers the dragon shall have his daughter to wife, and shall likewise govern the kingdom after his own death."

The huntsman said nothing more to this, but the next morning took his animals and with them ascended the dragon's hill. A little church stood at the top of it, and upon the altar were standing three full cups, with the inscription, "Whosoever empties the cups will become the strongest man on earth, and will be able to wield the sword which is buried before the threshold of the door." The huntsman did not drink, but went out and sought the sword in the ground. He was unable to move it from its place. Then he went in and emptied the cups, and now he was strong enough to take up the sword, and his hand could quite easily wield it.

When the hour came that the maiden was to be delivered over to the dragon, the king, the marshal, and courtiers accompanied her. From afar she saw the huntsman on the dragon's hill. She thought it was the dragon standing there waiting for her, and did not want to go up to him. But at last, because otherwise the whole town would have been destroyed, she was forced to make the miserable journey. The king and courtiers returned home full of grief. The king's marshal, however, was to stand still, and see all that transpired from a distance.

When the king's daughter got to the top of the hill, it was not the dragon which stood there, but the young huntsman, who comforted her and said he would save her. He led her into the church and locked her in. It was not long before the seven-headed dragon came forth with loud roaring. When he perceived the huntsman, he was astonished and said, "What business have you here on the hill?"

The huntsman answered, "I want to fight with you."

Said the dragon, "Many knights have left their lives here, I shall soon have made an end of you, too," and he breathed fire out of seven jaws. The fire was to have lighted the dry grass, and the huntsman was to have been suffocated in the heat and smoke, but his animals came running up and trampled out the fire.

Then the dragon rushed upon the huntsman, but he swung his sword until it sang through the air and struck off three of the dragon's heads. Then the dragon grew furious, rose up in the air, and spat out flames of fire over the huntsman. He was about to plunge down upon him, but the huntsman once more drew out his sword and again cut off three of his heads. The monster became faint and sank down, nevertheless he was just able to rush upon the huntsman. The huntsman, with his last strength, smote the dragon's tail off, and as he could fight no longer, called up his animals who tore the monster into pieces.

When the struggle was ended, the huntsman unlocked the church and found the king's daughter lying upon the floor, senseless from anguish and terror. He carried her out, and when she came to herself once more and opened her eyes, he showed her the dragon all cut to pieces and told her that she was now delivered.

She rejoiced and said, "Now you will be my dearest husband, for my father has promised me to him who kills the dragon." Thereupon she took off her necklace of coral and divided it amongst the animals in order to reward them, and the lion received the golden clasp. Her pocket handkerchief, however, upon which was her name, she gave to the huntsman, who went and cut the tongues out of the dragon's seven heads, wrapped them in the handkerchief, and preserved them carefully.

That done, as he was so exhausted with the fire and the battle, he said to the maiden, "We are both faint and weary. We will sleep awhile." She agreed, and they lay down on the ground. The huntsman said to the lion, "You must keep watch that no one surprises us in our sleep," and both he and the maiden fell asleep. The lion lay down beside them to watch, but he also was so weary with the fight that he called to the bear and said, "Lie down near me, I must sleep a little. If anything comes, waken me."

Then the bear lay down beside him, but he also was tired. He called the wolf and said, "Lie down by me. I must sleep a little, but if anything comes, waken me."

Then the wolf lay down by him, but he was tired likewise, so he called the fox and said, "Lie down by me. I must sleep a little. If anything comes, waken me."

Then the fox lay down beside him, but he, too, was weary, so he called the hare and said, "Lie down near me. I must sleep a little, and if anything should come, waken me."

Then the hare sat down by him, but the poor hare was

tired, too, and had no one whom he could call there to keep watch, and fell asleep. And now the king's daughter, the huntsman, the lion, the bear, the wolf, the fox, and the hare were all sleeping a sound sleep.

The marshal, however, who was to look on from a distance, took courage when he did not see the dragon flying away with the maiden, and, finding that all the hill had become quiet, ascended it. There lay the dragon hacked and hewn to pieces upon the ground, and not far from it were the king's daughter and a huntsman with his animals, and all of them were sunk in a sound sleep. As he was wicked and godless he took his sword, cut off the huntsman's head, seized the maiden in his arms, and carried her down the hill. Then she awoke and was terrified, but the marshal said, "You are in my hands. You shall say that it was I who killed the dragon."

"I cannot do that," she replied, "for it was a huntsman with his animals who did it."

Then he drew his sword and threatened to kill her if she did not obey him, and so compelled her that she promised it. Then he took her to the king, who did not know how to contain himself for joy when he once more looked upon his dear child in life, whom he had believed to have been torn to pieces by the monster.

The marshal said to him, "I have killed the dragon and delivered the maiden and the whole kingdom as well, therefore I demand her as my wife, as was promised."

The king said to the maiden, "Is what he says true?"

"Ah, yes," she answered, "it must indeed be true, but I will not consent to have the wedding celebrated until after a year and a day," for she thought in that time she should hear something of her dear huntsman.

The animals, meanwhile, were still lying sleeping beside their dead master upon the dragon's hill, and there came a great bumblebee and lighted upon the hare's nose, but the hare wiped it off with his paw and went on sleeping. The bumblebee came a second time, but the hare again rubbed it off and slept on. Then it came for the third time and stung his nose so that he awoke. As soon as the hare was awake, he roused the fox, and the fox the wolf, and the wolf the bear, and the bear the lion.

And when the lion awoke and saw that the maiden was gone and his master was dead, he began to roar frightfully and cried, "Who has done that? Bear, why did you not waken me?" The bear asked the wolf, "Why did you not waken me?" and the wolf the fox, "Why did you not waken me?" and the fox the hare, "Why did you not waken me?" The poor hare alone did not know what answer to make, and the blame rested with him.

Then they were just going to fall upon him, but he entreated them and said, "Kill me not, I will bring our master to life again. I know a mountain upon which a root grows, which, when placed in the mouth of anyone, cures him of all illness and every wound. But the mountain lies two hundred hours journey from here."

The lion said, "In four-and-twenty hours must you have run thither and have come back, and have brought the root with you."

Then the hare sprang away, and in four-and-twenty hours he was back and brought the root with him. The lion put the huntsman's head on again, and the hare placed the root in his mouth. Immediately everything united together again, and his heart beat, and life came back. Then the huntsman awoke, was alarmed when he did not see the maiden, and thought, *She must have gone away while I was sleeping in order to get rid of me.*

The lion in his great haste had put his master's head on the wrong way around, but the huntsman did not observe it because of his melancholy thoughts about the king's daughter. But at noon, when he was going to eat something, he saw that his head was turned backward and could not understand it, and asked the animals what had happened to him in his sleep.

Then the lion told him that they, too, had all fallen asleep from weariness. On awaking, they had found him dead with his head cut off, the hare had brought the life-giving root, and he, in his haste, had laid hold of the head the wrong way, but that he would repair his mistake. Then he tore the huntsman's head off again, turned it around, and the hare healed it with the root.

The huntsman, however, was sad at heart. He traveled about the world and made his animals dance before people. It came to pass that precisely at the end of one year he came back to the same town where he had delivered the king's daughter from the dragon, and this time the town was gaily hung with red cloth. He said to the host, "What does this mean? Last year the town was all hung with black crepe. What means the red cloth today?"

The host answered, "Last year our king's daughter was to have been delivered over to the dragon, but the marshal fought with it and killed it, and so tomorrow their wedding is to be solemnized. And that is why the town was then hung with black crepe for mourning, and is today covered with red cloth for joy."

The next day, when the wedding was to take place, the huntsman said at midday to the innkeeper, "Do you believe, sir host, that I while with you here today shall eat bread from the king's own table?"

"Nay," said the host, "I would bet a hundred pieces of gold that that will not come true." The huntsman accepted the wager and set against it a purse with just the same number of gold pieces. Then he called the hare and said, "Go, my dear runner, and fetch me some of the bread which the king is eating."

Now the little hare was the lowest of the animals and could not transfer this order to any of the others, but had to get upon his legs himself. *Alas!* thought he. *If I bound through the streets thus alone, the butchers' dogs will all be after me.*

It happened as he expected, and the dogs came after him and wanted to make holes in his good skin. But he sprang away and sheltered himself in a sentry box without the soldier being aware of it. Then the dogs came and wanted to have him out, but the soldier did not understand and struck them with the butt of his gun till they ran away yelling and howling.

As soon as the hare saw that the way was clear, he ran into

the palace and straight to the king's daughter, sat down under her chair, and scratched at her foot. She said, "Get away!" and thought it was her dog. The hare scratched her foot for the second time, and she again said, "Get away!" and thought it was her dog. But the hare did not let itself be turned from its purpose and scratched her for the third time. Then she peeped down and knew the hare by its collar. She took him upon her lap, carried him into her chamber, and said, "Dear hare, what do you want?"

He answered, "My master, who killed the dragon, is here, and has sent me to ask for a loaf of bread like that which the king eats."

Then she was full of joy, and had the baker summoned and ordered him to bring a loaf such as was eaten by the king.

The little hare said, "But the baker must likewise carry it there for me so that the butchers' dogs may do no harm to me." The baker carried it for him as far as the door of the inn, and then the hare got upon his hind legs, took the loaf in his front paws, and carried it to his master.

Then said the huntsman, "Behold, sir host, the hundred pieces of gold are mine." The host was astonished, but the huntsman went on to say, "Yes, sir host, I have the bread, but now I will likewise have some of the king's roast meat."

The host said, "I should indeed like to see that," but he would make no more wagers.

The huntsman called the fox and said, "My little fox, go and fetch me some roast meat such as the king eats." The red fox knew the byways better, and went by holes and corners without any dog seeing him, seated himself under the chair of the king's daughter and scratched her foot. She looked down and recognized the fox by its collar, took him into her chamber with her, and said, "Dear fox, what do you want?"

He answered, "My master, who killed the dragon, is here, and has sent me. I am to ask for some roast meat such as the king is eating." Then she made the cook prepare a roast joint, the same as was eaten by the king, and carry it for the fox as far as the door. Then the fox took the dish, waved away with his tail the flies which had settled upon the meat, and then carried it to his master.

"Behold, sir host," said the huntsman, "bread and meat are here, but now I will also have proper vegetables with it, such as are eaten by the king." Then he called the wolf, and said, "Dear wolf, go thither and fetch me vegetables such as the king eats."

Then the wolf went straight to the palace, as he feared no one, and when he got to the king's daughter's chamber, he twitched at the back of her dress so that she was forced to look around. She recognized him by his collar, took him into her chamber with her, and said, "Dear wolf, what do you want?"

He answered, "My master, who killed the dragon, is here, I am to ask for some vegetables such as the king eats." Then she made the cook come, and he had to make ready a dish of vegetables such as the king ate, and had to carry it for the wolf as far as the door. Then the wolf took the dish from him and carried it to his master.

"Behold, sir host," said the huntsman, "now I have bread

and meat and vegetables, but I will also have some pastry to eat such as the king eats." He called the bear, and said, "Dear bear, you are fond of licking anything sweet. Go and bring me some confectionery such as the king eats."

Then the bear trotted to the palace, and everyone got out of his way. But when he went to the guard, they presented their muskets and would not let him go into the royal palace. But he got up on his hind legs and gave them a few boxes on the ears, right and left with his paws, so that the whole watch broke up. Then he went straight to the king's daughter, placed himself behind her, and growled a little. She looked behind her, knew the bear, bade him go into her room with her, and said, "Dear bear, what do you want?"

He answered, "My master, who killed the dragon, is here, and I am to ask for some confectionery such as the king eats."

Then she summoned her confectioner, who had to bake confectionery such as the king ate and carry it to the door for the bear. The bear first licked up the candies that had rolled down, and then he stood upright, took the dish, and carried it to his master.

"Behold, sir host," said the huntsman, "now I have bread, meat, vegetables, and confectionery, but I will drink wine also such as the king drinks." He called his lion to him and said, "Dear lion, you like to drink till you are intoxicated, go and fetch me some wine such as is drunk by the king."

Then the lion strode through the streets, and the people fled from him. When he came to the watch, they wanted to bar the way against him, but he did but roar once, and they all ran away. Then the lion went to the royal apartment and knocked at the door with his tail. The king's daughter came forth, and was almost afraid of the lion, but she knew him by the golden clasp of her necklace and bade him go with her into her chamber, and said, "Dear lion, what will you have?"

He answered, "My master, who killed the dragon, is here, and I am to ask for some wine such as is drunk by the king." Then she bade the cup bearer be called, who was to give the lion some wine like that which was drunk by the king. The lion said, "I will go with him and see that I get the right wine."

Then he went down with the cup bearer, and when they were below, the cup bearer wanted to draw him some of the common wine that was drunk by the king's servants, but the lion said, "Stop, I will taste the wine first." He drew half a measure and swallowed it down at one draught.

"No," said he, "that is not right."

The cup bearer looked at him askance, but went on, and was about to give him some out of another barrel which was for the king's marshal. The lion said, "Stop, let me taste the wine first." He drew half a measure and drank it.

"That is better, but still not right," said he.

Then the cup bearer grew angry and said, "How can a stupid animal like you understand wine?"

The lion gave him a blow behind the ears, which made him fall down by no means gently. When he had got up again, he conducted the lion quite silently into a little cellar apart, where the king's wine lay, from which no one else ever drank. The lion first drew half a measure and tried the wine, and then he said, "That may possibly be the right sort," and bade the cup bearer fill six bottles of it.

And now they went upstairs again, but when the lion came out of the cellar into the open air, he reeled here and there, and was rather drunk. The cup bearer was forced to carry the wine as far as the door for him, and then the lion took the handle of the basket in his mouth and took it to his master.

The huntsman said, "Behold, sir host, here have I bread, meat, vegetables, confectionery, and wine such as the king has, and now I will dine with my animals." He sat down and ate and drank, and gave the hare, the fox, the wolf, the bear, and the lion also to eat and to drink, and was joyful, for he saw that the king's daughter still loved him.

When he had finished his dinner, he said, "Sir host, now have I eaten and drunk as the king eats and drinks, and now I will go to the king's court and marry the king's daughter."

Said the host, "How can that be, when she already has a betrothed husband, and when the wedding is to be solemnized today?"

Then the huntsman drew forth the handkerchief which the king's daughter had given him upon the dragon's hill and in which were folded the monster's seven tongues, and said, "That which I hold in my hand shall help me to do it."

Then the innkeeper looked at the handkerchief, and said, "Whatever I believe, I do not believe that, and I am willing to stake my house and courtyard upon it."

The huntsman, however, took a bag with a thousand gold pieces, put it upon the table, and said, "I stake that on it."

Now the king said to his daughter at the royal table, "What did all the wild animals want, which have been coming to you, and going in and out of my palace?"

She replied, "I may not tell you; but send and have the master of these animals brought, and you will do well."

The king sent a servant to the inn and invited the stranger, and the servant came just as the huntsman had laid his wager with the innkeeper. Then said he, "Behold, sir host, now the king sends his servant and invites me, but I do not go in this way." And he said to the servant, "I request the lord king to send me royal clothing, a carriage with six horses, and servants to attend me."

When the king heard the answer, he said to his daughter, "What shall I do?"

She said, "Cause him to be fetched as he desires to be, and you will do well."

Then the king sent royal apparel, a carriage with six horses, and servants to wait upon him. When the huntsman saw them coming, he said, "Behold, sir host, now I am fetched as I desired to be."

He put on the royal garments, took the handkerchief with the dragon's tongues with him, and drove off to the king. When the king saw him coming, he said to his daughter, "How shall I receive him?"

She answered, "Go to meet him and you will do well."

Then the king went to meet him and led him in, and his animals followed. The king gave him a seat near himself and his daughter. The marshal, as bridegroom, sat upon the other side, but no longer recognized the huntsman. At this very moment, the seven heads of the dragon were brought in as a spectacle, and the king said, "The seven heads were cut off the dragon by the marshal, wherefore today I give him my daughter to wife."

Then the huntsman stood up, opened the seven mouths, and said, "Where are the seven tongues of the dragon?"

Then was the marshal terrified, and he grew pale and knew not what answer he should make. At length in his anguish he said, "Dragons have no tongues."

The huntsman said, "Liars ought to have none, but the dragon's tongues are the tokens of the victor," and he unfolded the handkerchief, and there lay all seven inside it. And he put each tongue in the mouth to which it belonged, and it fitted exactly. Then he took the handkerchief upon which the name of the princess was embroidered, and showed it to the maiden and asked to whom she had given it. She replied, "To him who killed the dragon."

And then he called his animals, took the collar off each of them and the golden clasp from the lion, and showed them to the maiden and asked to whom they belonged.

She answered, "The necklace and golden clasp were mine, but I divided them among the animals who helped to conquer the dragon."

Then spoke the huntsman, "When I, tired with the fight, was resting and sleeping, the marshal came and cut off my head. Then he carried away the king's daughter and gave out that it was he who had killed the dragon. That he lied I prove with the tongues, the handkerchief, and the necklace." And then he related how his animals had healed him by means of a wonderful root, and how he had traveled about with them for one year, and had at length again come there and had learned the treachery of the marshal by the innkeeper's story.

Then the king asked his daughter, "Is it true that this man killed the dragon?"

And she answered, "Yes, it is true. Now can I reveal the wicked deed of the marshal, as it has come to light without my connivance, for he wrung from me a promise to be silent. For this reason, however, did I make the condition that the marriage should not be solemnized for a year and a day."

Then the king bade twelve councilors be summoned who were to pronounce judgment upon the marshal, and they sentenced him to be torn to pieces by four bulls. The marshal was therefore executed, and the king gave his daughter to the huntsman and named him his viceroy over the whole kingdom. The wedding was celebrated with great joy, and the young king caused his father and his foster father to be brought and loaded them with treasures.

Neither did he forget the innkeeper, but sent for him and said, "Behold, sir host, I have married the king's daughter, and your house and yard are mine."

The host said, "Yes, according to justice it is so."

But the young king said, "It shall be done according to mercy," and told him that he should keep his house and yard, and gave him the thousand pieces of gold as well.

And now the young king and queen were thoroughly happy and lived in gladness together. He often went out hunting because it was a delight to him, and the faithful animals had to accompany him. In the neighborhood, however, there was a forest of which it was reported that it was haunted, and that whosoever entered it did not easily get out again. The young king, however, had a great inclination to hunt in it, and let the old king have no peace until he allowed him to do so.

So he rode forth with a great following, and when he came to the forest, he saw a snow white hart and said to his people, "Wait here until I return. I want to chase that beautiful creature." He rode into the forest after it, followed only by his animals. The attendants halted and waited until evening, but he did not return, so they rode home and told the young queen that the young king had followed a white hart into the enchanted forest and had not come back again. Then she was in the greatest concern about him.

He, however, had still continued to ride on and on after the beautiful wild animal and had never been able to overtake it. When he thought he was near enough to aim, he instantly saw it bound away into the far distance, and at length it vanished altogether. And now he perceived that he had penetrated deep into the forest and blew his horn but he received no answer, for his attendants could not hear it. And as night was falling, he saw that he could not get home that day, so he dismounted from his horse, lighted himself a fire near a tree, and resolved to spend the night by it.

While he was sitting by the fire, and his animals also were lying down beside him, it seemed to him that he heard a human voice. He looked around, but could perceive nothing. Soon afterward, he again heard a groan as if from above, and then he looked up and saw an old woman sitting in the tree and wailing unceasingly, "Oh, oh, oh, how cold I am!"

"Come down, and warm yourself if you are cold," said the king.

But she replied, "No, your animals will bite me."

He answered, "They will do you no harm, old mother, do come down."

She, however, was a witch, and said, "I will throw down a wand from the tree, and if you strike them on the back with it, they will do me no harm."

Then she threw him a small wand, and he struck them with it. Instantly they lay still and were turned into stone. When the witch was safe from the animals, she leapt down and touched him also with a wand and changed him to stone. Thereupon she laughed and dragged him and the animals into a vault, in which many more such stones already lay.

When the young king did not come back at all, the queen's anguish and care grew constantly greater. It so happened that at this very time the other brother who had turned to the east when they separated came into the kingdom. He had sought a situation and had found none. He had then traveled about here and there and had made his animals dance. Then it came into his mind that he would just go and look at the knife that they had thrust in the trunk of a tree at their parting so that he might learn how his brother was. When he got there his brother's side of the knife was half rusted, and half bright. Then he was alarmed and thought, *A great misfortune must have befallen my brother, but perhaps I can still save him, for half the knife is still bright.*

He and his animals traveled toward the west. When he

entered the gate of the town, the guard came to meet him and asked if he was to announce him to his consort the young queen, who had for a couple of days been in the greatest sorrow about his staying away and was afraid he had been killed in the enchanted forest. The sentries, indeed, thought no otherwise than that he was the young king himself, for he looked so like him and had wild animals running behind him. Then he saw that they were speaking of his brother and thought, *It will be better if I pass myself off for him, and then I can rescue him more easily.*

So he allowed himself to be escorted into the castle by the guard and was received with the greatest joy. The young queen indeed thought that he was her husband and asked him why he had stayed away so long. He answered, "I had lost myself in a forest, and could not find my way out again any sooner."

At night he was taken to the royal bed, but he laid a two-edged sword between him and the young queen. She did not know what that could mean, but did not venture to ask.

He remained in the palace a couple of days, and in the meantime inquired into everything which related to the enchanted forest, and at last he said, "I must hunt there once more." The old king and the young queen wanted to persuade him not to do it, but he stood out against them and went forth with a larger following. When he had got into the forest, it fared with him as with his brother. He saw a white hart and said to his people, "Stay here, and wait until I return. I want to chase the lovely wild beast." And then he rode into the forest and his animals ran after him. But he could not overtake the hart and got so deep into the forest that he was forced to pass the night there. And when he had lighted a fire, he heard someone wailing above him, "Oh, oh, oh, how cold I am!" Then he looked up, and the self-same witch was sitting in the tree. Said he, "If you are cold, come down, little old mother, and warm yourself."

She answered, "No, your animals will bite me."

But he said, "They will not hurt you."

Then she cried, "I will throw down a wand to you, and if you smite them with it they will do me no harm."

When the huntsman heard that, he had no confidence in the old woman and said, "I will not strike my animals. Come down, or I will fetch you."

Then she cried, "What do you want? You shall not touch me."

But he replied, "If you do not come, I will shoot you."

Said she, "Shoot away, I do not fear your bullets!"

Then he aimed and fired at her, but the witch was proof against all leaden bullets, and she laughed, and yelled and cried, "You shall not hit me."

But the huntsman knew what to do. He tore three silver buttons off his coat, and loaded his gun with them, for against them her arts were useless. When he fired she fell down at once with a scream. Then he set his foot on her and said, "Old witch, if you do not instantly confess where my brother is, I will seize you with both my hands and throw you into the fire."

She was in a great fright and, begging for mercy, said, "He and his animals lie in a vault, turned to stone."

Then he compelled her to go there with him, threatened

her, and said, "Old monster, now you will make my brother and all the human beings lying here alive again, or you will go into the fire!"

She took a wand and touched the stones, and then his brother with his animals came to life again. Many others, merchants, artisans, and shepherds, arose, thanked him for their deliverance, and went to their homes. When the twin brothers saw each other again, they kissed each other and rejoiced with all their hearts. Then they seized the witch, bound her, and laid her upon the fire, and when she was burned the forest opened of its own accord, and was light and clear, and the king's palace could be seen at about the distance of a three-hour walk.

Thereupon the two brothers went home together, and on the way told each other their histories. And when the one said that he was ruler of the whole country in the king's stead, the other observed, "That I knew very well, for when I came to the town and was taken for you, all royal honors were paid me. The young queen looked upon me as her husband, and I had to eat at her side and sleep in your bed." When the other heard that, he became so jealous and angry that he drew his sword and struck off his brother's head. But when he saw him lying there dead and saw his red blood flowing, he repented most violently. "My brother delivered me!" cried he. "And I have killed him for it!" And he bewailed him aloud. Then his hare came, offered to go and bring some of the root of life, and bounded away and brought it while yet there was time. The dead man was brought to life again and knew nothing about the wound.

After this they journeyed onward, and the one said, "You look like me, have royal apparel on as I have, and the animals follow you as they do me. We will go in by opposite gates and arrive at the same time from the two sides in the aged king's presence."

So they separated, and at the same time came the watchmen from the one door and from the other and announced that the young king and the animals had returned from the chase. The king said, "It is not possible, the gates lie quite a mile apart."

In the meantime, however, the two brothers entered the courtyard of the palace from opposite sides, and both mounted the steps. Then the king said to the daughter, "Say which is your husband. Each of them looks exactly like the other, I cannot tell." Then she was in great distress and could not tell. But at last she remembered the necklace which she had given to the animals, and she sought for and found her little golden clasp on the lion, and she cried in her delight, "He who is followed by this lion is my true husband!" Then the young king laughed and said, "Yes, he is the right one."

They sat down together to table, and ate and drank, and were merry. At night when the young king went to bed, his wife said, "Why have you for these last nights always laid a two-edged sword in our bed? I thought you had a wish to kill me." Then he knew how true his brother had been.

THE SIX SERVANTS

❧

N former times there lived an aged queen who was a sorceress, and her daughter was the most beautiful maiden under the sun. The old woman, however, had no other thought than how to lure mankind to destruction, and when a wooer appeared, she said that whosoever wished to have her daughter must first perform three tasks, or die. Many had been dazzled by the daughter's beauty and had verily risked this, but they never could accomplish what the old woman enjoined them to do, and then no mercy was shown. They had to kneel down, and their heads were struck off.

A certain king's son, who had also heard of the maiden's beauty, said to his father, "Let me go there. I want to demand her in marriage."

"Never," answered the king. "If you were to go, it would be going to your death."

Upon this the son lay down and was sick unto death. For seven years he lay there, and no physician could heal him. When the father perceived that all hope was over, with a heavy heart he said to his son, "Go thither, and try your luck, for I know no other means of curing you."

When the son heard that, he rose from his bed and was well again, and joyfully set out on his way.

It came to pass that, as he was riding across a heath, he saw from afar something like a great heap of hay lying on the ground. When he drew nearer, he could see that it was the stomach of a man, who had laid himself down there, but the stomach looked like a small mountain. When the fat man saw the traveler, he stood up and said, "If you are in need of anyone, take me into your service."

The prince answered, "What can I do with such a great big man?"

"Oh," said the Stout One, "this is nothing. When I stretch myself out well, I am three thousand times fatter."

"If that's the case," said the prince, "I can make use of you, come with me."

So the Stout One followed the prince, and after a while they found another man who was lying upon the ground with his ear laid to the turf.

"What are you doing there?" asked the king's son.

"I am listening," replied the man.

"What are you listening to so attentively?"

"I am listening to what is just going on in the world, for nothing escapes my ears. I even hear the grass growing."

"Tell me," said the prince, "what you hear at the court of the old queen who has the beautiful daughter."

He answered, "I hear the whizzing of the sword that is striking off a wooer's head."

The king's son said, "I can make use of you. Come with me."

They went onward, and then saw, lying on the ground, a pair of feet and part of a pair of legs so long that they could not see the rest of the body. When they had walked on for a great distance, they came to the body, and at last to the head also.

"Why," said the prince, "what a tall rascal you are!"

"Oh," replied the Tall One, "that is nothing at all yet. When I really stretch out my limbs, I am three thousand times as tall, taller than the highest mountain on earth. I will gladly enter your service, if you will take me."

"Come with me," said the prince. "I can make use of you."

They went onward and found a man sitting by the road who had bound up his eyes. The prince said to him, "Are your eyes so weak that you cannot look at the light?"

"No," replied the man, "but I must not remove the bandage, for whatsoever I look at with my eyes splits to pieces, my glance is so powerful. If you can use that, I shall be glad to serve you."

"Come with me," replied the king's son. "I can make use of you."

They journeyed onward and found a man who was lying in the hot sunshine, trembling and shivering all over his body, so that not a limb was still.

"How can you shiver when the sun is shining so warm?" said the king's son.

"Alas," replied the man, "I am of quite a different nature. The hotter it is, the colder I am, and the frost pierces through all my bones. The colder it is, the hotter I am. In the midst of ice, I cannot endure the heat, nor in the midst of fire, the cold."

"You are a strange fellow," said the prince, "but if you will enter my service, follow me."

They traveled onward and saw a man standing who stretched his long neck and looked about him, and could see over all the mountains.

"What are you looking at so eagerly?" said the king's son.

The man replied, "I have such sharp eyes that I can see into every forest and field, and hill and valley, all over the world."

The prince said, "Come with me if you want, for I am still in want of someone like you."

And now the king's son and his six servants came to the town where the aged queen dwelt. He did not tell her who he was, but said, "If you will give me your beautiful daughter, I will perform any task you set me."

The sorceress was delighted to get such a handsome youth as this into her net, and said, "I will set you three tasks, and if you are able to perform them all, you will be husband and master of my daughter."

"What is the first to be?"

"You shall fetch me my ring which I have dropped into the Red Sea."

So the king's son went home to his servants and said, "The first task is not easy. A ring is to be got out of the Red Sea. Come, find some way of doing it."

Then the man with the sharp sight said, "I will see where it is lying," and looked down into the water and said, "It is sticking there, upon a pointed stone."

The Tall One carried them thither and said, "I would soon

get it out, if I could only see it."

"Oh, is that all!" cried the Stout One. He lay down and put his mouth to the water, and all the waves washed into it just as if it had been a whirlpool, and he drank up the whole sea till it was as dry as a meadow. Then the Tall One stooped down a little, and brought out the ring with his hand. The king's son rejoiced when he had the ring, and took it to the old queen.

She was astonished, and said, "Yes, it is the right ring. You have safely performed the first task, but now comes the second. Do you see the meadow in front of my palace? Three hundred fat oxen are feeding there. You must eat them all—skin, hair, bones, and horns. And down below in my cellar lie three hundred casks of wine, and these you must drink up as well. If one hair of the oxen or one little drop of the wine is left, your life will be forfeited to me."

"May I invite no guests to this repast?" inquired the prince. "No dinner is good without some company."

The old woman laughed maliciously, and replied, "You may invite one for the sake of companionship, but no more."

The king's son went to his servants and said to the Stout One, "You shall be my guest today and shall eat your fill."

Hereupon the Stout One stretched himself out and ate the three hundred oxen without leaving one single hair, and then he asked if he was to have nothing but his breakfast. He drank the wine straight from the casks without feeling any need of a glass, and he licked the last drop from his fingers.

When the meal was over, the prince went to the old

woman and told her that the second task also was performed. She wondered at this and said, "No one has ever done so much before, but one task still remains." She then thought to herself, *You shall not escape me and will not keep your head on your shoulders!*

"This night," said she, "I will bring my daughter to you in your chamber, and you shall put your arms around her. But when you are sitting there together, beware of falling asleep. When twelve o'clock is striking, I will come, and if she is then no longer in your arms, you are lost."

The prince thought, *The task is easy. I will most certainly keep my eyes open.*

Nevertheless he called his servants, told them what the old woman had said, and remarked, "Who knows what treachery lurks behind this? Foresight is a good thing. Keep watch, and take care that the maiden does not go out of my room."

When night fell, the old woman came with her daughter and gave her into the prince's arms. The Tall One then wound himself around the two in a circle, and the Stout One placed himself by the door, so that no living creature could enter. There the two sat, and the maiden spoke never a word. The moon shone through the window upon her face, and the prince could behold her wondrous beauty. He did nothing but gaze at her, filled with love and happiness, and his eyes never felt weary. This lasted until eleven o'clock, when the old woman cast such a spell over all of them that they fell asleep, and at the same moment the maiden was carried away.

They all slept soundly until a quarter to twelve, when the magic lost its power and all awoke again.

"Oh, misery and misfortune!" cried the prince. "Now I am lost!"

The faithful servants also began to lament, but the Listener said, "Be quiet, I want to listen." Then he listened for an instant and said, "She is on a rock, three hundred leagues from hence, bewailing her fate. You alone, Tall One, can help her. If you will stand up, you will be there in a couple of steps."

"Yes," answered the Tall One, "but Sharp Eyes must go with me so that we may destroy the rock."

Then the Tall One took the one with bandaged eyes on his back, and in the twinkling of an eye they were on the enchanted rock. The Tall One immediately took the bandage from the other's eyes, and he did but look around, and the rock shivered into a thousand pieces. Then the Tall One took the maiden in his arms, carried her back in a second, then fetched his companion with the same rapidity. Before the clock struck twelve they were all sitting as they had sat before, quite merrily and happily.

When twelve struck, the aged sorceress came stealing in with a malicious face, which seemed to say, "Now he is mine!" for she believed that her daughter was upon the rock three hundred leagues off. But when she saw her in the prince's arms, she was alarmed, and said, "Here is one who knows more than I do!" She dared not make any opposition and was forced to give him her daughter. But she whispered in her daughter's ear, "It is a disgrace to you to have to obey common people, and that you are not allowed to choose a husband to your own liking."

On this the proud heart of the maiden was filled with anger, and she meditated revenge. The next morning she caused three hundred great bundles of wood to be got together, and said to the prince that though the three tasks were performed, she would still not be his wife until someone was ready to seat himself in the midst of the wood and bear the fire. She thought that none of his servants would let themselves be burned for him, and that out of love for her, he himself would place himself upon it, and then she would be free.

But the servants said, "Every one of us has done something except the Frosty One, he must set to work," and they put him in the middle of the pile and set fire to it. Then the fire began to burn, and burned for three days until all the wood was consumed. When the flames had burnt out, the Frosty One was standing amid the ashes, trembling like an aspen leaf, and saying, "I never felt such a frost during the whole course of my life! If it had lasted much longer, I should have been frozen!"

As no other pretext was to be found, the beautiful maiden was now forced to take the unknown youth as a husband. But when they drove away to church, the old woman said, "I cannot endure the disgrace." She sent her warriors after them with orders to cut down all who opposed them and bring back her daughter.

But the Listener had sharpened his ears and heard the secret discourse of the old woman. "What shall we do?" said he to the Stout One.

But the Stout One knew what to do, and spat out once or

twice behind the carriage some of the seawater which he had drunk, and a great sea arose in which the warriors were caught and drowned. When the sorceress perceived that, she sent her knights. But the Listener heard the rattling of their armor, and undid the bandage from one eye of Sharp Eyes, who looked for a while rather fixedly at the enemy's troops, upon which they all broke into pieces like glass. Then the youth and the maiden went upon their way undisturbed.

When the two had been blessed in church, the six servants took leave, and said to their master, "Your wishes are now satisfied. You need us no longer. We will go our way and seek our fortunes."

Half a league from the palace of the prince's father was a village near which a swineherder tended his herd. When they came there the prince said to his wife, "Do you know who I really am? I am no prince, but a herder of swine, and the man who is there with that herd is my father. We two shall have to set to work also and help him."

Then he alighted with her at the inn and secretly told the innkeepers to take away her royal apparel during the night. When she awoke in the morning, she had nothing to put on. The innkeeper's wife gave her an old gown and a pair of worsted stockings, which at the same time she seemed to consider a great favor, and said, "If it were not for the sake of your husband I should have given you nothing at all!"

Then the princess believed that he really was a swineherder and tended the herd with him, and she thought to herself, *I have deserved this for my haughtiness and pride.*

This lasted for a week, until she could endure it no longer, for she had sores on her feet. And now came several towns-people who asked if she knew who her husband was.

"Yes," she answered, "he is a swineherder and has just gone out with cords and ropes to try to drive a little bargain."

But they said, "Just come with us, and we will take you to him." They took her up to the palace, and when she entered the hall, there stood her husband in kingly raiment. But she did not recognize him until he took her in his arms, kissed her, and said, "I suffered much for you and now you, too, have had to suffer for me." And then the wedding was cele-brated, and he who has told you all this, wishes that he, too, had been present at it.

THE OLD WOMAN
IN THE WOOD

⚜

POOR servant-girl was once traveling through a great forest with the family with which she was in service. When they were in the midst of it, robbers came out of the thicket and murdered all they found. All perished together except the girl, who had jumped out of the carriage in a fright and hidden herself behind a tree. When the robbers had gone away with their booty, she came out and beheld the great disaster. Then she began to weep bitterly and said, "What can a poor girl like me do now? I do not know how to get out of the forest, no human being lives in it, so I must certainly starve."

She walked about and looked for a road, but could find none. When it was evening she seated herself under a tree, gave herself into God's keeping, and resolved to sit waiting there and not go away, whatever might befall her. When, however, she had sat there for a while, a white dove came flying to her with a little golden key in its mouth. It put the little key in her hand and said, "Do you see that great tree? Inside it is a little lock. It opens with the tiny key, and there you will find food enough and suffer no more hunger." She went to the tree and opened it, and found milk in a little dish and white bread to dip in it. When she had eaten her fill, she said, "It is now the time when the hens at home go to roost, I am so tired I could go to bed, too."

Then the dove flew to her again, and brought another golden key in its bill, and said, "Open that tree there, and you will find a bed." So she opened it and found a beautiful white bed. She prayed God to protect her during the night, and lay down and slept.

In the morning the dove came for the third time and again brought a little key, and said, "Open that tree there, and you will find clothes." And when she opened it, she found garments beset with gold and with jewels, more splendid than those of any king's daughter.

So she lived there for some time, and the dove came every day and provided her with all she needed, and it was a quiet good life.

Once, however, the dove came and said, "Will you do something for my sake?"

"With all my heart," said the girl.

Then said the little dove, "I will guide you to a small house. Enter it, and inside it, an old woman will be sitting by the fire and will say, 'Good day.' But upon your life give her no answer, let her do what she will, but pass by her upon the right side. Further on, there is a door, which you must open, and you will enter into a room where a quantity of rings of all kinds are lying, amongst which are some magnificent ones with shining stones. Leave them, however, where they are, and seek out a plain one, which must likewise be amongst them, and bring it here to me as quickly as you can."

The girl went to the little house and came to the door. There sat an old woman who stared when she saw her, and said, "Good day, my child." The girl gave her no answer and opened the door.

"Where are you going?" cried the old woman. She seized the girl by her gown and tried to hold her fast, saying, "That is my house. No one can go in there if I choose not to allow it."

But the girl was silent, got away from her, and went straight into the room.

Now there lay on the table an enormous quantity of rings, which gleamed and glittered before her eyes. She turned them over and looked for the plain one, but could not find it. While she was seeking, she saw that the old woman was trying to sneak off with a birdcage. So the girl went after her and took the cage out of her hand. When she looked into the cage, a bird was inside with the plain ring in its bill.

Then she took the ring and ran quite joyously home with it, thinking the little white dove would come for the ring. But it did not come. Then she leaned against a tree and determined to wait for the dove. As she thus stood, it seemed just as if the tree was soft and pliant, and was letting its branches down. Suddenly the branches twined around her and were two arms. When she looked around, the tree was a handsome man, who embraced and kissed her heartily, and said, "You have delivered me from the power of the old woman, who is a wicked witch. She had changed me into a tree, and every day for two hours I was a white dove, and so long as she possessed the ring I could not regain my human form."

Then his servants and his horses, who had likewise been changed into trees, were freed from the enchantment also, and stood beside him. And he led them forth to his kingdom, for he was a king's son, and they married and lived happily.

THE ROBBER BRIDEGROOM

✤

HERE was once upon a time a miller who had a beautiful daughter. When she was grown up, he wished that she was provided for and well married. He thought, *If any good suitor comes and asks for her, I will give her to him.* Not long afterward, a suitor who appeared to be very rich came, and as the miller had no fault to find with him, he promised his daughter to him.

The maiden, however, did not like him quite so much as a girl should like the man to whom she is engaged, and had no confidence in him. Whenever she saw or thought of him, she felt a secret horror. Once he said to her, "You are my betrothed, and yet you have never once paid me a visit."

The maiden replied, "I know not where your house is."

Then said the bridegroom, "My house is out there in the dark forest."

She tried to excuse herself and said she could not find the way there. The bridegroom said, "Next Sunday you must come out there to me. I have already invited the guests, and I will strew ashes in order that you may find your way through the forest."

When Sunday came and the maiden had to set out on her

way, she became very uneasy, though she herself knew not exactly why. To mark her way she filled both her pockets full of peas and lentils. Ashes were strewn at the entrance of the forest, and these she followed, but at every step she threw a couple of peas upon the ground.

She walked almost the whole day until she reached the middle of the forest, where it was the darkest. There stood a solitary house, which she did not like, for it looked so dark and dismal. She went inside it, but no one was within, and the most absolute stillness reigned. Suddenly a voice cried,

> *"Turn back, turn back, young maiden dear,*
> *'Tis a murderer's house you enter here!"*

The maiden looked up, and saw that the voice came from a bird hanging in a cage upon the wall. Again it cried,

> *"Turn back, turn back, young maiden dear,*
> *'Tis a murderer's house you enter here!"*

Then the young maiden went on farther from one room to another and walked through the whole house, but it was entirely empty and not one human being was to be found. At last she came to the cellar, and there sat an extremely aged woman, whose head shook constantly.

"Can you not tell me," said the maiden, "if my betrothed lives here?"

"Alas, poor child," replied the old woman, "why have you

come? You are in a murderer's den. You think you are a bride soon to be married, but you will keep your wedding with death. Look, I have been forced to put a great kettle on there with water in it. When they have you in their power, they will cut you to pieces without mercy, will cook you, and eat you, for they are eaters of human flesh. If I do not have compassion on you and save you, you are lost."

Thereupon the old woman led her behind a great hogshead where she could not be seen.

"Be as still as a mouse," said she, "do not make a sound, or move, or all will be over with you. At night, when the robbers are asleep, we will escape. I have long waited for an opportunity."

Hardly had she finished speaking when the wicked crew came home. They dragged with them another young girl. They were drunk and paid no heed to her screams and lamentations. They gave her three glasses full of wine to drink, one glass of white, one glass of red, and one glass of yellow, and with this her heart burst in two. Thereupon they laid her on a table, cut her in pieces, and strewed salt on her.

The poor bride behind the cask trembled and shook, for she saw clearly what fate the robbers had destined for her.

One of them noticed a gold ring upon the little finger of the murdered girl, and as it would not come off at once, he took an axe and cut the finger off. It sprang up in the air, away over the cask and fell straight into the bride's lap. The robber took a candle and wanted to look for it, but could not find it. Then another of them said, "Have you looked behind the great hogshead?" But the old woman cried, "Come and get something to eat, and leave off looking till the morning, the finger won't run away from you."

Then the robbers said, "The old woman is right," and gave up their search. As they sat sat down to eat, the old woman poured a sleeping draught in their wine, so that they soon lay down in the cellar, and slept and snored. When the bride heard that, she came out from behind the hogshead and had to step over the sleepers, for they lay in rows upon the ground. Great was her terror lest she should waken one of them! But God helped her, and she got safely over. The old woman went up with her, opened the doors, and they hurried out of the murderers' den with all the speed in their power. The wind had blown away the strewn ashes, but the peas and lentils had sprouted and grown up, and showed them the way in the moonlight. They walked the whole night, until in the morning they arrived at the mill. Then the maiden told her father everything exactly as it had happened.

When the day came when the wedding was to be celebrated, the bridegroom appeared at the mill as if nothing had happened. The miller had invited all his relations and friends. As they sat at the table, each was bidden to relate something. The bride sat still and said nothing. Then said the bridegroom to the bride, "Come, my darling, do you know nothing? Relate something to us like the rest."

She replied, "Then I will relate a dream. I was walking alone through a wood. At last I came to a house, in which no living soul was, but on the wall there was a bird in a cage which cried,

'Turn back, turn back, young maiden dear,
'Tis a murderer's house you enter here!'

And this it cried once more. My darling, I only dreamt this. Then I went through all the rooms, and they were all empty, but there was something so horrible about them! At last I went down into the cellar, and there sat an old woman, whose head shook. I asked her, 'Does my bridegroom live in this house?' She answered, 'Alas, poor child, you have got into a murderer's den, your bridegroom does live here, but he will hew you in pieces, and kill you, and then he will cook you, and eat you.' My darling, I only dreamt this. But the old woman then hid me behind a great hogshead. Scarcely was I hidden when the robbers came home, dragging a maiden with them, to whom they gave three kinds of wine to drink— white, red, and yellow—with which her heart broke in two. My darling, I only dreamt this. Thereupon they hewed her fair body in pieces upon a table and sprinkled them with salt. My darling, I only dreamt this. One of the robbers saw that there was still a ring on her little finger, and as it was hard to draw off, he took an axe and cut it off. But the finger sprang up in the air, behind the great hogshead, and fell into my lap. And there is the finger with the ring!" With these words she drew it forth and showed it to those present.

The robber, who had during this story become as pale as ashes, leapt up and wanted to escape, but the guests held him fast and delivered him over to justice. Then he and his whole troop were executed for their infamous deeds.

ROLAND AND MAYBIRD

HERE was once a poor man who went every day to cut wood in the forest. One day, as he went along he heard a cry like a little child's. He followed the sound till at last he looked up a high tree, and upon one of the branches sat a very little girl. Her mother had fallen asleep, and a vulture had taken the girl out of her lap, flown away with her, and left her on the tree. Then the woodcutter climbed up, took the little child down, and said to himself, "I will take this poor child home and bring her up with my own son Roland." So he brought her to his cottage, and both grew up together. He called the little girl Maybird, because he had found her upon a tree in May. Maybird and Roland were so very fond of each other that they were never happy but when they were together.

But the woodcutter became very poor and had nothing in the world he could call his own. Indeed he had scarcely bread enough for his wife and the two children to eat. At last the time came when even that was all gone, and he knew not where to seek for help in his need. Then at night, as he lay upon his bed and turned himself here and there, restless and full of care, his wife said to him, "Husband, listen to me. Take the two children out early tomorrow morning. Give each of them a piece of bread, and then lead them into the midst of the wood where it is thickest, make a fire for them, and go away and leave them alone to shift for themselves, for we can no longer keep them here."

"No, wife," said the husband. "I cannot find it in my heart to leave the children to the wild beasts of the forest that would soon tear them to pieces."

"Well, if you will not do as I say," answered the wife, "we must starve together." She let him have no peace until he agreed to her plan.

Meanwhile, the poor children, too, were lying awake restless and weak from hunger, so that they heard all that their mother said to her husband. *Now,* thought Maybird to herself, *it is all up with us,* and she began to weep. But Roland crept to her bedside and said, "Do not be afraid, Maybird, I will find out some help for us." Then he got up, put on his jacket, opened the door, and went out.

The moon shone bright upon the little court before the cottage, and the white pebbles glittered like daisies upon the green meadows. So he stooped down, put as many as he could into his pocket, and then went back to the house. "Now, Maybird," said he, "rest quietly," and he went to bed and fell fast asleep.

Early in the morning, before the sun had risen, the woodcutter's wife came and awoke them. "Get up, children," said she. "We are going into the wood. There is a piece of bread for each of thee, but take care of it and keep some for the afternoon." Maybird took the bread and carried it in her apron, because Roland had his pocket full of stones, and they made their way into the wood.

After they had walked on for a time, Roland stood still and looked toward home, and after a while turned again, and so on several times. Then his father said, "Roland, why do you keep turning and lagging about so? Move your legs on a little faster."

"Ah! Father," answered Roland, "I am stopping to look at my white cat that sits upon the roof and wants to say good-bye to me."

"You little fool!" said his mother. "That is not your cat. 'Tis the morning sun shining upon the chimney top." Now Roland had not been looking at the cat, but had all the while been staying behind to drop from his pocket one white pebble after another along the road.

When they came into the midst of the wood, the woodcutter said, "Run about, children, and pick up some wood, and I will make a fire to keep us all warm."

So they piled up a little heap of brushwood, and set it afire. As the flame burned bright, the mother said, "Now set yourselves by the fire and go to sleep, while we go and cut wood in the forest. Be sure you wait till we come again and fetch you."

Roland and Maybird sat by the fireside till the afternoon, and then each of them ate their piece of bread. They fancied the woodcutter was still in the wood, because they thought they heard the blows of his axe. But it was a bough which he had cunningly hung upon a tree, so that the wind blew it backward and forward, and it sounded like the axe as it hit the other boughs. Thus, they waited till evening, but the wood-cutter and his wife kept away, and no one came to fetch them.

When it was quite dark Maybird began to cry, but Roland said, "Wait a while till the moon rises." And when the moon rose, he took her by the hand, and there lay the pebbles along the ground, glittering like new pieces of money and marking the way out. Toward morning they came again to the woodcutter's house, and he was glad in his heart when he saw the children again, for he had grieved at leaving them alone. His wife also seemed to be glad, but in her heart she was angry .

Not long after there was again no bread in the house, and Maybird and Roland heard the wife say to her husband, "The children found their way back once, and I took it in good part. But there is only half a loaf of bread left for them in the house. Tomorrow you must take them deeper into the wood that they may not find their way out, or we shall all be starved."

It grieved the husband in his heart to do as his wife wished, and he thought it would be better to share their last morsel with the children. But as he had done as she said once, he did not dare to say no. When the children had heard all their plan, Roland got up and wanted to pick up pebbles as before, but when he came to the door he found his mother had locked it. Still he comforted Maybird and said, "Sleep in peace, dear Maybird. God is very kind and will help us."

Early in the morning a piece of bread was given to each of them, but smaller than the one they had before. Upon the road Roland crumbled his in his pocket, and often stood still and threw a crumb upon the ground.

"Why do you lag so behind, Roland?" said the woodcutter. "Go on ahead."

"I am looking at my little dove that is sitting upon the roof and wants to say good-bye to me."

"You silly boy!" said the wife. "That is not your little dove, it is the morning sun that shines upon the chimney top."

But Roland went on crumbling his bread and throwing it upon the ground. And thus they went on still farther into the wood, where they had never been before in all their lives. There they were again told to sit down by a large fire, and sleep. The woodcutter and his wife said they would come in the evening and fetch them away. In the afternoon Roland shared Maybird's bread, because he had strewed all his upon the road. But the day passed away, and evening passed away, too, and no one came to the poor children. Still Roland comforted Maybird and said, "Wait till the moon rises. Then I shall see the crumbs of bread which I have strewed, and they will show us the way home."

The moon rose, but when Roland looked for the crumbs, they were gone, for thousands of little birds in the wood had found them and picked them up. Roland set out to try and find their way home, but they were soon lost in the wilderness. They went on through the night and all the next day, till at last they lay down and fell asleep for weariness. Another day they went on as before, but still did not reach the end of the wood, and were as hungry as could be, for they had nothing to eat.

In the afternoon of the third day they came to a strange little hut made of bread, with a roof of cake, and windows of sparkling sugar. "Now we will sit down and eat till we have had enough," said Roland. "I will eat off the roof for my share. Eat the windows, Maybird. They will be nice and sweet for you." While Maybird was picking at the sugar, however, a sweet pretty voice called from within,

"Tip, tap! Who goes there?"

But the children answered,

"The wind, the wind,
That blows through the air"

and went on eating. Maybird broke out a round pane of the window for herself, and Roland tore off a large piece of cake from the roof, when the door opened, and a little old fairy came gliding out. At this Maybird and Roland were so frightened that they let fall what they had in their hands. But the old lady shook her head and said, "Dear children, where have you been wandering about? Come in with me. You shall have something good."

So she took them both by the hand and led them into her little hut. Then she brought out plenty to eat—milk and pancakes with sugar, apples, and nuts. And then two beautiful little beds were got ready, and Maybird and Roland laid themselves down and thought they were in heaven.

But the fairy was a spiteful one and had made her pretty sweetmeat house to entrap little children. Early in the morning, before they were awake, she went to their little beds, and when she saw the two sleeping and looking so sweetly, she had no pity on them, but was glad they were in her power. Then she took up Roland and put him in a little cage by himself. When he awoke, he found himself behind a grating, shut up as little chickens are. She shook Maybird and called out, "Get up, you lazy little thing, and fetch some water. Go into the kitchen and cook something good to eat. Your brother is shut up yonder. I shall first fatten him, and when he is fat, I think I shall eat him."

When the fairy was gone, the little girl got up and ran to Roland, told him what she had heard, and said, "We must run away quickly, for the old woman is a bad fairy and will kill us."

But Roland said, "You must first steal away her fairy wand so that we may save ourselves if she should follow."

The little maiden ran back to fetch the magic wand, and away they went together. When the old fairy came back, she could see no one at home. She sprang in a great rage to the window and looked out into the wide world (which she could do far and near). A long way off she spied Maybird running away with her dear Roland. "You are already a great way off," said she, "but you will still fall into my hands."

Then she put on her boots which walked several miles at a step, and scarcely made two steps with them before she overtook the children. Maybird saw that the fairy was coming after them, and by the help of the wand turned her dear Roland into a lake and herself into a swan which swam about in the middle of it.

The fairy set herself down upon the shore and took a great deal of trouble to entice the swan. She threw crumbs of bread to it, but it would not come near her, and she was forced to go home in the evening without taking her revenge.

Maybird changed herself and her dear Roland back into their own forms once more, and they went journeying on the whole night until the dawn of day. Then the maiden turned herself into a beautiful rose, which grew in the midst of a quickset hedge, and Roland sat by its side and played upon his flute.

The fairy soon came striding along. "Good piper," said she, "may I pluck the beautiful rose for myself?"

"Oh, yes," answered he, "and I will play to you meantime."

So when she had crept into the hedge in a great hurry to gather the flower, for she well knew who it was, he began to play upon his flute. Whether she liked it or not, such was the wonderful power of the music that she was forced to dance a merry jig, on and on without any rest. And as he did not cease playing a moment, the thorns at length tore the clothes from off her body, pricked her sorely, and there she stuck quite fast.

Then Maybird was free once more, but she was very tired. Roland said, "Now I will hasten home for help, and by and by we will be married."

And Maybird said, "I will stay here in the meantime and wait for you. That no one may know me, I will turn myself into a stone and lie in the corner of yonder field."

Then Roland went away, and Maybird was to wait for him. But Roland met with another maiden, who pleased him so much that he stopped where she lived and forgot his former love. When Maybird had stayed in the field a long time and found he did not come back, she became quite sorrowful and turned herself into a little daisy. She thought to herself, *Someone will come and tread me under foot, and so my sorrows will end.*

But it so happened that as a shepherd was keeping watch in the field. He found the flower and, thinking it very pretty, took it home, placed it in a box in his room, and said, "I have never found so pretty a flower before."

From that time everything throve wonderfully at the shepherd's house. When he got up in the morning, all the housework was already done, the room was swept and cleaned, the fire made, and the water fetched. In the afternoon, when he came home, the tablecloth was laid and a good dinner ready for him. He could not make out how all this happened, for he saw no one in his house. Although it pleased him well enough, he was at length troubled to think how it could be. He went to a cunning woman who lived nearby and asked her what he should do. She said, "There must be witchcraft in it. Look out tomorrow morning early, and see if anything stirs about in the room. If it does, throw a white cloth at once over it and then the witchcraft will be stopped."

The shepherd did as she said, and the next morning saw the box open and the daisy come out. He sprang up quickly and threw a white cloth over it. In an instant the spell was broken, and Maybird stood before him, for it was she who had taken care of his house for him. As she was so beautiful he asked her if she would marry him. She said, "No," because she wished to be faithful to her dear Roland. But she agreed to stay and keep house for him.

Time passed on, and Roland was to be married to the

maiden whom he had found. According to an old custom in that land, all the maidens were to come and sing songs in praise of the bride and bridegroom. But Maybird was so grieved when she heard that her dearest Roland had forgotten her and was to be married to another, that her heart seemed as if it would burst within her, and she would not go for a long time.

At length she was forced to go with the rest, but she kept hiding herself behind the others until she was left the last. Then she could not any longer help coming forward. The moment she began to sing, Roland sprang up and cried out, "That is my true bride; I will have no other but her," for he knew her by the sound of her voice. All that he had forgotten came back into his mind, and his heart was opened toward her.

So faithful Maybird was married to her dear Roland, and there was an end of her sorrows. From that time forward she lived happily till she died.

THE TWELVE BROTHERS

✣

HERE were once on a time a king and a queen who lived happily together and had twelve children, but they were all boys. Then said the king to his wife, "If the thirteenth child which you are about to bring into the world is a girl, the twelve boys shall die, in order that her possessions may be great and that the kingdom may fall to her alone." He caused likewise twelve coffins to be made, which were already filled with shavings, and in each lay the little pillow for the dead. He had them taken into a locked-up room, and then he gave the queen the key of it and bade her not to speak of this to anyone.

The mother, however, now sat and lamented all day long, until the youngest son, Benjamin, who was always with her and whose name she had taken from the Bible, said to her, "Dear mother, why are you so sad?"

"Dearest child," she answered, "I may not tell you." But he let her have no rest until she went and unlocked the room and showed him the twelve coffins filled with shavings. Then she said, "My dearest Benjamin, your father has had these coffins made for you and for your eleven brothers, for if I bring a little girl into the world, you are all to be killed and buried in them."

And as she wept while she was saying this, the son comforted her and said, "Weep not, dear mother, we will save ourselves, and go hence."

But she said, "Go forth into the forest with your eleven brothers. Let one sit constantly upon the highest tree which can be found and keep watch, looking toward the tower here in the castle. If I give birth to a little son, I will put up a white flag, and then you may venture to come back. But if I bear a daughter, I will hoist a red flag, and then fly hence as quickly as you are able, and may the good God protect you. Every night I will rise up and pray for you—in winter that you may be able to warm yourself at a fire, and in summer that you may not faint away in the heat."

After she had blessed her sons therefore, they went forth into the forest. They each kept watch in turn by sitting on the highest oak and looking toward the tower. When eleven days had passed and the turn came to Benjamin, he saw that a flag was being raised. It was, however, not the white, but the bloodred flag which announced that they were all to die. When the brothers heard that, they were very angry and said, "Are we all to suffer death for the sake of a girl? We swear that we will avenge ourselves! Wheresoever we find a girl, her red blood shall flow."

Thereupon they went deeper into the forest, and in the midst of it where it was the darkest, they found a little bewitched hut, which was standing empty. Then said they,

"Here we will dwell, and you Benjamin, who are the youngest and weakest, you shall stay at home and keep house. We
others will go out and get food." Then they went into the forest and shot hares, wild deer, birds, pigeons, and whatsoever
there was to eat. This they took to Benjamin, who had to
dress it for them in order that they might appease their
hunger. They lived together ten years in the little hut, and the
time did not appear long to them.

The little daughter whom their mother the queen had
given birth to was now grown up. She was good of heart, fair
of face, and had a golden star on her forehead. Once, when it
was the great washing, she saw twelve men's shirts amongst
the things and asked her mother, "To whom do these twelve
shirts belong, for they are far too small for Father?"

Then the queen answered with a heavy heart, "Dear child,
these belong to your twelve brothers."

Said the maiden, "Where are my twelve brothers, I have
never yet heard of them?"

She replied, "God knows where they are, they are wandering about the world." Then she took the maiden and opened
the chamber for her, and showed her the twelve coffins with
the shavings and pillows for the head. "These coffins," said
she, "were destined for your brothers, but they went away
secretly before you were born," and she related to her how
everything had happened. Then said the maiden, "Dear
mother, weep not, I will go and seek my brothers."

So she took the twelve shirts and went forth straight into
the great forest. She walked the whole day, and in the evening

she came to the bewitched hut. She entered it and found a young boy, who asked, "Where have you come from and where are you bound?" He was astonished that she was so beautiful, wore royal garments, and had a star on her forehead.

And she answered, "I am a king's daughter and am seeking my twelve brothers, and I will walk as far as the sky is blue until I find them."

She likewise showed him the twelve shirts which belonged to them. Then Benjamin saw that she was his sister, and said, "I am Benjamin, your youngest brother." And she began to weep for joy, and Benjamin wept also, and they kissed and embraced each other with the greatest love.

But after this he said, "Dear sister, there is still one difficulty. We have agreed that every maiden whom we meet shall die, because we have been obliged to leave our kingdom on account of a girl." Then said she, "I will willingly die if by so doing I can deliver my twelve brothers."

"No," answered he, "you shall not die, seat yourself beneath this tub until our eleven brothers come, and then I will soon come to an agreement with them."

She did so, and when it was night the others came from hunting, and their dinner was ready. As they were sitting at table and eating, they asked, "What news is there?"

Said Benjamin, "Don't you know anything?"

"No," they answered.

He continued, "You have been in the forest and I have stayed at home, and yet I know more than you do."

"Tell us then!" they cried.

He answered, "But promise me that the first maiden who meets us shall not be killed."

"Yes!" they all cried. "She shall have mercy, only do tell us!"

Then said he, "Our sister is here." He lifted up the tub, and the king's daughter came forth in her royal garments with the golden star on her forehead. She was beautiful, delicate, and fair. Then they all rejoiced and fell on her neck, and kissed and loved her with all their hearts.

Now she stayed at home with Benjamin and helped him with the work. The eleven went into the forest and caught game, deer, birds, and woodpigeons that they might have food, and the little sister and Benjamin took care to make it ready for them. She sought for the wood for cooking and herbs for vegetables, and put the pans upon the fire so that the dinner was always ready when the eleven came. She likewise kept order in the little house and put beautifully white clean coverings upon the little beds, and the brothers were always contented and lived in great harmony with her.

Once on a time the two at home had prepared a beautiful entertainment, and when they were all together, they sat down and ate and drank and were full of gladness. There was, however, a little garden belonging to the bewitched house wherein stood twelve lily flowers. She wished to give her brothers pleasure and plucked the twelve flowers, and thought she would present each brother with one while at dinner.

But at the very moment that she plucked the flowers the twelve brothers were changed into twelve ravens, and flew away over the forest and the house and garden vanished like-wise. And now the poor maiden was alone in the wild forest. When she looked around, an old woman was standing near her, who said, "My child, what have you done? Why did you not leave the twelve white flowers growing? They were your brothers, who are now for evermore changed into ravens."

The maiden said, weeping, "Is there no way of delivering them?"

"No," said the woman, "there is but one way in the whole world, and that is so hard that you will not deliver them by it, for you must be dumb for seven years. You may not speak or laugh. If you speak but a single word, and only an hour of the seven years is wanting, all is in vain, and your brothers will be killed by the one word."

Then said the maiden in her heart, *I know with certainty that I shall set my brothers free.* She went and sought a high tree and seated herself in it and span, and neither spoke nor laughed.

Now it so happened that a king was hunting in the forest, and he had a great grayhound which ran to the tree upon which the maiden was sitting and sprang about it, whining and barking at her. Then the king came by and saw the princess with the golden star upon her brow, and was so charmed with her beauty that he called to ask her if she would be his wife. She made no answer, but nodded a little with her head. So he climbed up the tree himself, carried her down, placed her upon his horse, and bore her home.

Then the wedding was solemnized with great magnifi-cence and rejoicing, but the bride neither spoke nor smiled. When they had lived happily together for a few years, the king's stepmother, who was a wicked woman, began to slander the young queen, and said to the king, "This is a common beggar-girl whom you have brought back with you. Who knows what impious tricks she practices secretly! Even if she be dumb and not able to speak, she still might laugh for once. Those who do not laugh have bad consciences."

At first the king would not believe it, but the old woman urged this so long, and accused her of so many evil things, that at last the king let himself be persuaded and sentenced his wife to death.

A great fire was lighted in the courtyard in which she was to be burned. The king stood above at the window and looked on with tearful eyes, because he still loved her so much. When she was bound fast to the stake, and the fire was licking at her clothes with its red tongue, the last instant of the seven years expired. Then a whirring sound was heard in the air, and twelve ravens came flying toward the place and sank downward. When they touched the earth they were her twelve brothers, whom she had delivered. They tore the fire asunder, extinguished the flames, set their dear sister free, and kissed and embraced her. And now as she dared to open her mouth and speak, she told the king why she had been dumb and had never laughed. The king rejoiced when he heard that she was innocent, and they all lived in great unity until their death. The wicked stepmother was taken before the judge, put into a barrel filled with boiling oil and venomous snakes, and died an evil death.

THE PEASANT'S WISE
DAUGHTER

✤

HERE was once a poor peasant who had no land, but only a small house and one daughter. Then said the daughter, "We ought to ask our lord the king for a bit of newly cleared land."

When the king heard of their poverty, he presented them with a piece of land, which she and her father dug up and intended to sow with a little corn and other grains. When they had dug nearly the whole of the field, they found in the earth a mortar made of pure gold.

"Listen," said the father to the girl, "as our lord the king has been so gracious and presented us with the field, we ought to give him this mortar in return for it."

The daughter, however, would not consent to this, and said, "Father, if we have the mortar without having the pestle as well, we shall have to get the pestle, so you had much better say nothing about it."

He would, however, not obey her, but took the mortar and carried it to the king, said that he had found it in the cleared land, and asked if he would accept it as a present. The king took the mortar, and asked if he had found nothing besides that. "No," answered the countryman. Then the king said that he must now bring him the pestle. The peasant said they had not found that, but he might just as well have spoken to the wind.

He was put in prison, and was to stay there until he produced the pestle. The servants had daily to carry him bread and water, which is what people get in prison, and they heard how the man cried out continually, "Ah! If I had but listened to my daughter! Alas, alas, if I had but listened to my daughter!" He would neither eat nor drink.

So the king commanded the servants to bring the prisoner before him, and then he asked the peasant why he was always crying. "Ah! If I had but listened to my daughter!" The peasant told the king what his daughter had said. "She told me that I ought not to take the mortar to you, for I should have to produce the pestle as well."

"If you have a daughter who is as wise as that, let her come here."

She was therefore obliged to appear before the king, who asked her if she really was so wise and said he would set her a riddle. If she could guess the riddle, he would marry her. She at once said yes, she would guess it.

Then said the king, "Come to me not clothed, not naked, not riding, not walking, not in the road, and not out of the road, and if you can do that I will marry you."

So she went away, and took off everything she had on so that she was not clothed. Next, she took a great fishing net, seated herself in it, and wrapped it entirely around and around her, so that she was not naked. She hired a donkey and tied the fisherman's net to its tail, so that it was forced to drag her along, and that was neither riding nor walking. The ass had also to drag her in the ruts so that she only touched the ground with her big toe, and that was neither being in the road nor out of the road.

And when she arrived in that fashion, the king said she had guessed the riddle and fulfilled all the conditions. Then he ordered her father to be released from the prison, took her as his wife, and gave into her care all the royal possessions.

Now when some years had passed, the king was once drawing up his troops on parade, when it happened that some peasants who had been selling wood stopped with their wagons before the palace. Some of them had oxen yoked to them, and some had horses.

There was one peasant who had three horses, one of which was delivered of a young foal, and it ran away and lay down between two oxen which were hitched to another peasant's wagon. When the two peasants came together, they began to agree, beating each other and making a disturbance. The peasant with the oxen wanted to keep the foal and said one of the oxen had given birth to it. The other said his horse had had it, and that it was his.

The quarrel came before the king, and he give the verdict that the foal should stay where it had been found, and so the peasant with the oxen, to whom it did not belong, got it. Then the other went away, and wept and lamented over his foal.

Now this peasant had heard how gracious his lady the queen was because she herself had sprung from poor peasant folks, so he went to her and begged her to see if she could not help him to get his foal back again. Said she, "Yes, I will tell you what to do, if you will promise me not to betray me. Early tomorrow morning, when the king parades the guard, place yourself there in the middle of the road by which he must pass, take a great fishing net and pretend to be fishing. Go on fishing, too, and empty out the net as if you had got it full." Then she told him also what he was to say if he was questioned by the king.

The next day, therefore, the peasant stood there and fished upon dry ground. When the king passed by and saw that, he sent his messenger to ask what the stupid man was about.

The peasant answered, "I am fishing." The messenger asked how he could fish when there was no water there.

The peasant said, "It is as easy for me to fish upon dry land as it is for an ox to have a foal."

The messenger went back and took the answer to the king, who ordered the peasant to be brought to him. The king recognized that this was not the peasant's own idea, and he wanted to know at once whose it was. The peasant, however, would not talk and said always that the idea was his own. So they laid him upon a heap of straw and beat him and tormented him so long that at last he admitted that he had got the idea from the queen.

When the king reached home again, he said to his wife, "Why have you behaved so falsely to me? I will not have you any longer for a wife. Your time is up, go back to the place from whence you came, to your peasant's hut."

One favor, however, he granted her. She might take with her the one thing that was dearest and best in her eyes, and thus was she dismissed.

She said, "Yes, my dear husband, if you command this, I will do it," and she embraced him and kissed him, and asked him to drink her health.

Then she ordered a powerful sleeping draught to be brought. The king took a long draught, but she took only a little. He soon fell into a deep sleep, and when she perceived that, she called a servant and took a fair white linen cloth and wrapped the king in it. The servant was forced to carry him into a carriage that stood before the door, and she drove with him to her own little house. She laid him in her own little bed, and he slept one day and one night without awakening. When he awoke he looked around and said, "Good God! Where am I?" He called his attendants, but none of them were there.

At length his wife came to his bedside and said, "My dear lord and king, you told me I might bring away with me from the palace that which was dearest and most precious in my eyes. I have nothing more precious and dear than yourself, so I have brought you with me."

Tears rose to the king's eyes and he said, "Dear wife, you shall be mine and I will be yours." He took her back with him to the royal palace and was married again to her, and at the present time they are very likely still living.

THE DEVIL AND HIS
GRANDMOTHER

❧

HERE was a great war, and the king had many soldiers but gave them small pay, so small that they could not live upon it, so three of them agreed amongst themselves to desert.

One of them said to the others, "If we are caught we shall be hanged upon the gallows. How shall we manage it?"

Another said, "Look at that great cornfield. If we were to hide ourselves there, no one could find us. The troops are not allowed to enter it, and tomorrow they are to march away."

The deserters crept into the corn—only the troops did not march away, but remained lying all around about it. They stayed in the corn for two days and two nights and were so hungry that they all but died, but if they had come out, their death would have been certain. Then said they, "What is the use of our deserting if we have to perish miserably here?"

But now a fiery dragon came flying through the air, and it came down to them and asked why they had concealed themselves there. They answered, "We are three soldiers who have deserted because the pay was so bad, and now we shall have to die of hunger if we stay here or to dangle on the gallows if we go out."

"If you will serve me for seven years," said the dragon, "I will convey you through the army so that no one shall seize you."

"We have no choice and are compelled to accept," they replied.

Then the dragon caught hold of them with his claws, carried them away through the air over the army, and put them down again on the earth far from it. But the dragon was none other than the devil. He gave them a small whip and said, "Whip with it and crack it, and then as much gold will spring up as you can wish for. Then you can live like great lords, keep horses, and drive your carriages, but when the seven years have come to an end, you are my property." Then he put before them a book which they were all three forced to sign. "I will, however, then set you a riddle," said he, "and if you can guess that, you shall be free, and released from my power."

Then the dragon flew away from them, and they went away with their whip, had gold in plenty, ordered themselves rich apparel, and traveled about the world. Wherever they were they lived in pleasure and magnificence, rode upon horseback, drove in carriages, ate and drank, but did nothing wicked. The time slipped quickly away, and when the seven years were coming to an end, two of them were terribly anxious and alarmed. But the third took the affair easily and said, "Brothers, fear nothing, my head is sharp enough. I shall guess the riddle."

They all went out into the open country where they sat down, and the two made sorrowful faces. Then an aged woman came up to them who inquired why they were so sad. "Alas!" said they. "How can that concern you? After all, you cannot help us."

"Who knows?" said she. "Confide your trouble to me."

So they told her that they had been the devil's servants for nearly seven years, and that he had provided them with gold as plentifully as if it had been blackberries. But they had sold themselves to him and were forfeited to him if at the end of the seven years they could not guess a riddle.

The old woman said, "If you are to be saved, one of you must go into the forest. There he will come to a fallen rock which looks like a little house. He must enter that, and then he will obtain help."

The two melancholy ones thought to themselves, "That will still not save us," and stayed where they were. But the third, the merry one, got up and walked on into the forest until he found the rock-house. In the little house was sitting a very aged woman who was the devil's grandmother. She asked the soldier where he came from and what he wanted there. He told her everything that had happened, and as he pleased her well, she had pity on him and said she would help him. She lifted up a great stone which lay above a cellar and said, "Conceal yourself there. You can hear everything that is said here. Only sit still, and do not stir. When the dragon comes, I will question him about the riddle. He tells everything to me, so listen carefully to his answer."

At twelve o'clock at night, the dragon came flying and asked for his dinner. The grandmother laid the table and served up food and drink so that he was pleased, and they ate and drank together. In the course of conversation, she asked him what kind of a day he had had, and how many souls he had got. "Nothing went very well today," he answered, "but I have laid hold of three soldiers. I have them safe."

"Indeed! Three soldiers, that's something, but they may escape you yet."

The devil said mockingly, "They are mine! I will set them a riddle, which they will never in this world be able to guess!"

"What riddle is that?" she inquired.

"I will tell you. In the great North Sea lies a dead monkey that shall be their roast meat, and the rib of a whale shall be their silver spoon, and a hollow old horse's hoof shall be their wineglass."

When the devil had gone to bed, the old grandmother raised up the stone and let out the soldier. "Have you paid particular attention to everything?"

"Yes," said he. "I know enough, and will contrive to save myself."

Then he had to go back another way, through the window, secretly and with all speed to his companions. He told them how the devil had been betrayed by the old grandmother and how he had learned the answer to the riddle from him. Then they were all joyous and of good cheer. They took the whip and whipped up so much gold for themselves that it ran all over the ground.

When the seven years had fully gone by, the devil came with the book, showed the signatures, and said, "I will take you with me to hell. There you shall have a meal! If you can guess what kind of roast meat you will have to eat, you shall be free and released from your bargain, and may keep the whip as well."

Then the first soldier began and said, "In the great North Sea lies a dead monkey that no doubt is the roast meat."

The devil was angry and began to mutter, "Hm! Hm! Hm!" And he asked the second soldier, "But what will your spoon be?"

"The rib of a whale is to be our silver spoon."

The devil made a wry face, again growled, "Hm! Hm! Hm!" and said to the third soldier, "And do you also know what your wineglass is to be?"

"An old horse's hoof is to be our wineglass."

Then the devil flew away with a loud cry and had no more power over them, but the three kept the whip, whipped up as much money for themselves with it as they wanted, and lived happily to their end.

THE TRUE BRIDE

HERE was once upon a time a girl who was young and beautiful, but she had lost her mother when she was quite a child, and her stepmother did all she could to make the girl's life wretched. Whenever this woman gave her anything to do, she worked at it indefatigably and did everything that lay in her power. Still, she could not touch the heart of the wicked woman. Her stepmother was never satisfied. The harder the girl worked, the more work was put upon her. Her stepmother thought only of how to weigh her down with still heavier burdens and make her life still more miserable.

One day she said to the girl, "Here are twelve pounds of feathers which you must pick, and if they are not done this evening, you may expect a good beating. Do you imagine you are to idle away the whole day?"

The poor girl sat down to the work, but tears ran down her cheeks as she did so, for she saw plainly enough that it was quite impossible to finish the work in one day. Whenever she had a little heap of feathers lying before her and she sighed or smote her hands together in her anguish, they flew away, and she had to pick them out again and begin her work anew.

Then she put her elbows upon the table, laid her face in her two hands, and cried, "Is there no one, then, on God's earth to have pity on me?"

Suddenly, she heard a low voice which said, "Be comforted, my child, I have come to help you."

The maiden looked up, and an old woman was by her side. She took the girl kindly by the hand and said, "Only tell me what is troubling you."

As she spoke so kindly, the girl told her of her miserable life, how one burden after another was laid upon her, and she never could get to the end of the work which was given to her. "If I have not done these feathers by this evening, my stepmother will beat me. She has threatened she will, and I know she keeps her word." Her tears began to flow again, but the good old woman said, "Do not be afraid, my child. Rest a while, and in the meantime I will look to your work."

The girl lay down on her bed and soon fell asleep. The old woman seated herself at the table with the feathers, and how they did fly off the quills, which she scarcely touched with her withered hands! The twelve pounds were soon finished, and when the girl awoke, great snow-white heaps were lying, piled up, and everything in the room was neatly cleared away, but the old woman had vanished. The maiden thanked God and sat still till evening came, when the stepmother came in and marveled to see the work completed.

"Just look, you awkward creature," said she, "what can be done when people are industrious. Why could you not set about something else? There you sit with your hands crossed." When she went out, she said, "The creature is worth more than her salt. I must give her some work that is still harder."

The next morning she called the girl and said, "There is a spoon for you. With that you must empty out for me the great pond which is beside the garden, and if it is not done by night, you know what will happen."

The girl took the spoon and saw that it was full of holes. But even if it had not been, she never could have emptied the pond with it. She set to work at once, knelt down by the water, into which her tears were falling, and began to empty it.

But the good old woman appeared again, and when she learnt the cause of the girl's grief, she said, "Be of good cheer, my child. Go into the thicket and lie down and sleep. I will soon do your work." As soon as the old woman was alone, she barely touched the pond, and a vapor rose up on high from the water and mingled itself with the clouds. Gradually the pond was emptied, and when the maiden awoke before sunset and came thither, she saw nothing but the fish that were struggling in the mud. She went to her stepmother and showed her that the work was done.

"It ought to have been done long before this," said she, and grew white with anger, but she meditated something new.

On the third morning she said to the girl, "You must build me a castle on the plain there, and it must be ready by the evening."

The maiden was dismayed, and said, "How can I complete such a great work?"

"I will endure no opposition!" screamed the stepmother. "If you can empty a pond with a spoon that is full of holes, you can build a castle, too. I will take possession of it this very day, and if anything is wanting, even if it be the most trifling thing in the kitchen or cellar, you know what lies before you!"

She drove the girl out, and when the girl entered the valley, the rocks were there, piled up one above the other. She knew that all her strength would not have enabled her even to move the very smallest of them. She sat down and wept, and still she hoped the old woman would help her. The old woman was not long in coming. She comforted the girl and said, "Lie down there in the shade and sleep, and I will soon build the castle for you. If it would be a pleasure to you, you can live in it yourself."

When the maiden had gone away to sleep, the old woman touched the gray rocks. They began to rise, and immediately moved together as if giants had built the walls. On these the building arose, and it seemed as if countless hands were working invisibly, placing one stone upon another. There was a dull heavy noise from the ground. Pillars arose of their own accord on high and placed themselves in order near one another. The tiles laid themselves down upon the roof, and when noon came, the great weather vane was already turning itself on the summit of the tower, like a golden figure of the Virgin with fluttering garments.

The inside of the castle was being finished while evening was drawing near. How the old woman managed it, I know not, but the walls of the rooms were hung with silk and velvet, embroidered chairs were there, and richly ornamented armchairs sat by marble tables. Crystal chandeliers hung down from the ceilings and mirrored themselves in the smooth pavement. Green parrots were there in gilt cages, and so were strange birds which sang most beautifully, and there was on all sides as much magnificence as if a king were going to live there.

The sun was just setting when the girl awoke, and the brightness of a thousand lights flashed in her face. She hurried to the castle and entered by the open door. The steps were spread with red cloth, and the golden balustrade beset with flowering trees. When she saw the splendor of the apartment, she stood as if turned to stone. Who knows how long she might have stood there if she had not remembered the stepmother?

"Alas!" she said to herself. "If she could but be satisfied at last, and would give up making my life a misery to me."

The girl went and told her that the castle was ready.

"I will move into it at once," said she, and rose from her seat.

When they entered the castle, she was forced to hold her hand before her eyes, the brilliance of everything was so dazzling. "You see," said she to the girl, "how easy it has been for you to do this. I ought to have given you something harder." She went through all the rooms and examined every corner to see if anything was wanting or defective, but she could discover nothing.

"Now we will go down below," said she, looking at the girl with malicious eyes. "The kitchen and the cellar still have to be examined, and if you have forgotten anything you shall not escape your punishment."

But the fire was burning upon the hearth, the meat was

cooking in the pans, the tongs and shovel were leaning against the wall, and the shining brazen utensils all arranged in sight. Nothing was wanting, not even a coal box and water pail.

"Which is the way to the cellar?" she cried. "If that is not abundantly filled, it shall go ill with you."

She herself raised up the trapdoor and descended, but she had hardly made two steps before the heavy trapdoor, which was only propped back, fell down. The girl heard a scream and lifted up the door very quickly to go to her aid, but the stepmother had fallen down, and the girl found her lying lifeless at the bottom.

Now the magnificent castle belonged to the girl alone. She at first did not know how to reconcile herself to her good fortune. Beautiful dresses were hanging in the wardrobes, the chests were filled with gold or silver or with pearls and jewels, and she never felt a desire that she was not able to gratify. Soon the fame of the beauty and riches of the maiden went over all the world. Wooers presented themselves daily, but none pleased her. At length the son of the king came and he knew how to touch her heart, and she betrothed herself to him.

In the garden of the castle was a lime tree, under which they were one day sitting together, when he said to her, "I will go home and obtain my father's consent to our marriage. I entreat you to wait for me here under this lime tree, I shall be back with you in a few hours." The maiden kissed him upon his left cheek, and said, "Keep true to me, and never let anyone else kiss you upon this cheek. I will wait here under the lime tree until you return."

The maid stayed beneath the lime tree until sunset, but he did not return. She sat three days from morning till evening waiting for him, but in vain. As he still was not there by the fourth day, she said, "Some accident has assuredly befallen him. I will go out and seek him, and will not come back until I have found him." She packed up three of her most beautiful dresses, one embroidered with bright stars, the second with silver moons, the third with golden suns, tied up a handful of jewels in her handkerchief, and set out. She inquired everywhere for her betrothed, but no one had seen him. No one knew anything about him. Far and wide did she wander through the world, but she found him not. At last she hired herself to a farmer as a shepherdess, and buried her dresses and jewels beneath a stone.

And now she lived as a herdswoman, guarded her herd, and was very sad and full of longing for her beloved one. She had a little calf which she taught to know her and fed it out of her own hand, and when she said,

> *"Little calf, little calf, kneel by my side,*
> *And do not forget your dear shepherd-maid,*
> *As the prince forgot his betrothed bride,*
> *Who waited for him 'neath the lime tree's shade, "*

the little calf knelt down, and she petted it.

When she had lived for a few years alone and full of grief, a report was spread over all the land that the king's daughter was about to celebrate her marriage. The road to the town passed through the village where the maiden was living, and it came to pass that once when the maiden was driving out her herd, her bridegroom traveled by. He was sitting proudly on his horse and never looked around, but when she saw him she recognized her beloved, and it was just as if a sharp knife had pierced her heart. "Alas!" said she. "I believed him true to me, but he has forgotten me."

The next day he again came along the road. When he was near her, she said to the little calf,

> *"Little calf, little calf, kneel by my side,*
> *And do not forget your dear shepherd-maid,*
> *As the prince forgot his betrothed bride,*
> *Who waited for him 'neath the lime tree's shade."*

When he was aware of the voice, he looked down and reined in his horse. He looked into the maiden's face, and then put his hands before his eyes as if he were trying to remember something, but he soon rode onward and was out of sight. "Alas!" said she. "He no longer knows me," and her grief was ever greater.

Soon after this a great festival three days long was to be held at the king's court, and the whole country was invited to it.

Now will I try my last chance, thought the maiden, and when evening came she went to the stone under which she had buried her treasures. She took out the dress with the golden suns, put it on, and adorned herself with the jewels. She let down her hair, which she had concealed under a handkerchief, and it fell down in long curls about her. Thus she went into the town, and in the darkness was observed by no one.

When she entered the brightly lighted hall, everyone started back in amazement, but no one knew who she was. The king's son went to meet her, but he did not recognize her. He led her out to dance, and was so enchanted with her beauty that he thought no more of the other bride. When the feast was over, she vanished in the crowd and hastened before daybreak to the village, where she once more put on her herd's dress.

The next evening she took out the dress with the silver moons, and put a half-moon made of precious stones in her hair. When she appeared at the festival, all eyes were turned upon her. The king's son hastened to meet her and, filled with love for her, danced with her alone, and no longer so much as glanced at anyone else. Before she went away he made her promise to come again to the festival on the last evening.

When she appeared for the third time, she wore the star dress which sparkled at every step she took, and her hair ribbon and girdle were starred with jewels. The prince had already been waiting for her for a long time and made his way up to her.

"Do but tell me who you are," said he. "I feel just as if I had already known you a long time."

"Do you not know what I did when you left me?"

Then she stepped up to him, and kissed him upon his left cheek, and in a moment it was as if scales fell from his eyes, and he recognized his true bride.

"Come," said he to her, "here I stay no longer." He gave her his hand and led her down to the carriage. The horses hurried away to the magic castle as if the wind had been harnessed to the carriage. The illuminated windows already shone in the distance. When they drove past the lime tree, countless glow-worms were swarming about it. It shook its branches and sent forth their fragrance. Upon the steps flowers were blooming, and the room echoed with the song of strange birds. In the hall the entire court was assembled, and the priest was waiting to marry the bridegroom to the true bride.

JORINDA AND JORINGEL

❈

HERE was once an old castle in the midst of a large and dense forest, and in it an old woman who was a witch dwelt all alone. In the daytime she changed herself into a cat or a screech owl, but in the evening she took her proper shape again as a human being. She could lure wild beasts and birds to her, which she would kill, then boil or roast. If a man came within one hundred paces of the castle, she would cast a spell on him, making him frozen in place until she bade him be free. But whenever an innocent maiden came within this circle, she changed her into a bird, shut her up in a wickerwork cage, and carried the cage into a room in the castle. She had more than seven thousand cages of rare birds in the castle.

Now, there was once a maiden who was called Jorinda, who was fairer than all other girls. She and a handsome youth named Joringel had promised to marry each other. They were still in the days of betrothal, and their greatest happiness was being together. One day, in order that they might be able to talk together in peace, they went for a walk in the forest.

"Take care," said Joringel, "that you do not go too near the castle."

It was a beautiful evening. The sun shone brightly between the trunks of the trees into the dark green of the forest, and the turtledoves sang mournfully upon the beech trees.

Jorinda wept now and then. She sat down in the sunshine and was sorrowful. Joringel was sorrowful, too. They were as sad as if they were about to die. Then they looked around them and were quite at a loss, for they did not know by which way they should go home. The sun was still half above the mountain and half under. Joringel looked through the bushes and saw the old walls of the castle close at hand. He was horror-stricken and filled with deadly fear, while Jorinda sang:

> "My little bird, with the necklace red,
>   Sings sorrow, sorrow, sorrow,
>   He sings that the dove must soon be dead,
>   Sings sorrow, sor—oh, oh, oh."

Joringel looked for Jorinda. She was changed into a nightingale, and sang, *oh, oh, oh*. A screech owl with glowing eyes flew three times around about her and three times cried, *"To-whoo, To-whoo, To-whoo."*

Joringel could not move. He stood there like a stone and could neither weep nor speak, nor move hand or foot. The sun had now set. The owl flew into the thicket and directly afterward there came out of it a crooked old woman, yellow and lean, with large red eyes and a crooked nose, the point of which reached to her chin. She muttered to herself, caught the nightingale, and took it away in her hand. Still, Joringel could neither speak nor move from the spot. The nightingale was gone.

At last the woman came back and said in a hollow voice, "Greetings, Zachiel. When the moon shines upon the cage, Zachiel, let him loose at once."

Then Joringel was freed. He fell upon his knees before the woman and begged that she would give him back his Jorinda, but she said that he should never have her again and went away. He called, he wept, he lamented, but all in vain, "What is to become of me?"

Joringel went away and at last came to a strange village where he kept sheep for a long time. He often walked around and around the castle, but not too near to it. At last he dreamt one night that he found a bloodred flower, in the middle of which was a beautiful large pearl. He dreamt that he picked the flower and went with it to the castle, and that everything he touched with the flower was freed from enchantment. He also dreamt that by means of it he recovered his Jorinda. In the morning, when he awoke, he began to seek over hill and dale for such a flower. He sought it until the ninth day when, early in the morning, he found the bloodred flower. In the middle of it there was a large dewdrop, as big as the finest pearl.

Day and night he journeyed with this flower to the castle. When he was within a hundred paces of it, he was not held fast, but walked on to the door. Joringel was full of joy. He touched the door with the flower, and it sprang open. He walked in through the courtyard and listened for the sound of the birds. At last he heard them. He went on and found the room from whence the sound came, and there the witch was feeding the birds in the seven thousand cages.

When she saw Joringel she was very angry, and she scolded and spat poison and gall at him. But she could not come within two paces of him. He did not take any notice of her, but went and looked at the cages with the birds. There were many hundred nightingales. How was he to find his Jorinda again? Just then he saw the old woman quietly take away a cage with a bird in it and go toward the door.

Swiftly he sprang toward her, touched the cage with the flower, and also the old woman. She could now no longer bewitch anyone. And Jorinda was standing there, clasping him around the neck, and she was as beautiful as ever. Then all the other birds were turned into maidens again, and Joringel went home with his Jorinda, and they lived happily together for a long time.

FITCHER'S BIRD

✤

HERE was once a wizard who used to take the form of a poor man, and go begging from house to house so that he could catch pretty girls. No one knew where he took them, for they were never seen again.

One day, he appeared before the door of a man who had three pretty daughters. He looked like a poor weak beggar and carried a basket upon his back as if he meant to collect charitable gifts in it. He begged for a little food, and when the eldest daughter came out and was just handing him a piece of bread, he touched her, and she was forced to jump into his basket. Thereupon he hurried away with long strides, and carried her to his house in the midst of a dark forest.

Everything in the house was magnificent. He gave her whatsoever she could possibly desire and said, "My darling, you will certainly be happy with me, for you have everything your heart can wish for."

This lasted a few days, and then he said, "I must journey forth and leave you alone for a short time. There are the keys of the house. You may go everywhere and look at everything except one room, which this little key here opens. There I forbid you to go upon pain of death." He likewise gave her an egg and said, "Preserve the egg carefully for me, and carry it continually about with you, for a great misfortune would arise from the loss of it."

She took the keys and the egg, and promised to obey him in everything. When he was gone, she went all round the house from the bottom to the top and examined everything. The rooms shone with silver and gold, and she thought she had never seen such great splendor. At length she came to the forbidden door. She wished to pass it by, but curiosity let her have no rest. She examined the key. It looked just like any other. She put it in the keyhole and turned it a little, and the door sprang open. But what did she see when she went in? A great bloody basin stood in the middle of the room, and therein lay human beings, dead and hewn to pieces, and nearby was a block of wood, and a gleaming axe lay upon it. She was so terribly alarmed that the egg which she held in her hand fell into the basin. She got it out and washed the blood off, but in vain. The blood appeared again in a moment. She washed and scrubbed, but she could not get it out.

It was not long before the man came back from his journey, and the first things which he asked for were the key and the egg. She gave them to him, but she trembled as she did so, and he saw at once by the red spots that she had been in the bloody chamber.

"Since you have gone into the room against my will," said he, "you shall go back into it against your own. Your life is ended."

He threw her down, dragged her to the room by her hair,

cut her head off upon the block, and hewed her in pieces so that her blood ran upon the ground. Then he threw her into the basin with the rest.

"Now I will fetch myself the second," said the wizard. Again he went to the house in the shape of a poor man and begged. Then the second daughter brought him a piece of bread. He caught her like the first, by simply touching her, and carried her away. She did not fare better than her sister. She allowed herself to be led away by her curiosity, opened the door of the bloody chamber, looked in, and had to atone for it with her life upon the wizard's return.

Then he went and brought the third sister, but she was clever and crafty. When he had given her the keys and the egg and had left her, she first put the egg away with great care, and then she examined the house, and at last went into the forbidden room. Alas, what did she behold! Both her sisters lay there in the basin, cruelly murdered and cut into pieces. She didn't despair, but set to work to gather their limbs together and put them in order, head, body, arms, and legs. And when nothing further was wanting, the limbs began to move and unite themselves together, and both the maidens opened their eyes and were once more alive. Then they rejoiced and kissed and caressed one another.

On his arrival, the man at once demanded the keys and the egg, and as he could perceive no trace of any blood on it, he said, "You have stood the test. You shall be my bride." But after saying this, he no longer had any power over her, and was forced to do whatsoever she desired.

"Oh, very well," said she. "You shall first take a basketful of gold to my father and mother, and carry it yourself on your back. In the meantime, I will prepare for the wedding."

Then she ran to her sisters, whom she had hidden in a little chamber, and said, "The moment has come when I can save you. The wretch shall himself carry you home again, but as soon as you are at home send help to me." She put both of them in a basket and covered them quite over with gold, so that nothing of them was to be seen, then she called in the wizard and said to him, "Now carry the basket away, but I shall look through my little window and watch to see if you stop upon the way to stand or to rest."

The wizard raised the basket upon his back and went away with it, but it weighed him down so heavily that the perspiration streamed from his face. Then he sat down and wanted to rest a while, but immediately one of the girls in the basket cried, "I am looking through my little window, and I see that you are resting. Go on at once." He thought it was his bride who was calling that to him and got up on his legs again. Once more he was going to sit down, but instantly she cried, "I am looking through my little window, and I see that you are resting. Go on directly." And whenever he stood still, she cried this, and then he was forced to go onward, until at last, groaning and out of breath, he took the basket with the gold and the two maidens into their parents' house.

At the wizard's home, meanwhile, the bride prepared the marriage feast and sent invitations to the friends of the wizard. Then she took a skull with grinning teeth, put some ornaments and a wreath of flowers on it, carried it upstairs to the garret window, and let it look out from thence. When all was ready, she got into a barrel of honey, and then cut the featherbed open and rolled herself in it until she looked like a wondrous bird, and no one could recognize her. Then she went out of the house, and upon her way she met some of the wedding guests, who asked,

> "O, Fitcher's bird, how come you here?"
> "I come from Fitcher's house quite near."
> "And what may the young bride be doing?"
> "From cellar to garret she's swept all clean,
> And now from the window she's peeping, I ween."

At last she met the bridegroom, who was coming slowly back. He, like the others, asked,

> "O, Fitcher's bird, how come you here?"
> "I come from Fitcher's house quite near."
> "And what may the young bride be doing?
> "From cellar to garret she's swept all clean,
> And now from the window she's peeping, I ween."

The bridegroom looked up, saw the decked-out skull, thought it was his bride, and nodded to her, greeting her kindly. But when he and his guests had all gone into the house, the brothers and kinsmen of the bride, who had been sent to rescue her, arrived. They locked all the doors of the house that no one might escape and set fire to it, and the wizard and all his cohorts had to burn.

MOTHER HOLLE

❖

THERE was once a widow who had two daughters, one of whom was pretty and industrious, while the other was ugly and idle. But the widow was much fonder of the ugly and idle one because she was her own daughter. The other, who was a stepdaughter, was obliged to do all the work and to sweep the ashes of the house. Every day the poor girl had to sit by a well near the road, and spin and spin till her fingers bled.

Now it happened that one day the shuttle was dirtied with her blood, so she dipped it in the well to wash the mark off, but it dropped out of her hand and fell to the bottom. She began to weep, and ran to her stepmother and told her of the mishap. But the stepmother scolded her sharply and in her cruelty commanded: "Since you have let the shuttle fall in, you must fetch it out again."

So the girl went back to the well and did not know what to do. In the sorrow of her heart she jumped into the well to get the shuttle. She lost her senses, and when she awoke and came to herself again, she was in a lovely meadow where the sun was shining and many thousands of flowers were growing. Along this meadow she went, and at last came to a baker's oven full of bread. The bread cried out, "Oh, take me out! Take me out or I shall burn. I have been baked a long time!" So she went up to it, and took out all the loaves one after another with the bread shovel.

After that, she went on till she came to a tree covered with apples, which called out to her, "Oh, shake me! Shake me! We apples are all ripe!" So she shook the tree till the apples fell like rain and went on shaking till they were all down. When she had gathered them into a heap, she went on her way.

At last she came to a little house, out of which an old woman peeped. This woman had such large teeth that the girl was frightened and was about to run away. But the old woman called out to her, "What are you afraid of, dear child? Stay with me. If you will do all the work in the house properly, you shall be the better for it. Only you must take care to make my bed well, and to shake it thoroughly till the feathers fly, for then there is snow upon the earth. I am Mother Holle."

Since the old woman spoke so kindly to her, the girl took courage and agreed to enter her service. She attended to everything to the satisfaction of her mistress and always shook her bed so vigorously that the feathers flew about like snowflakes. So she had a pleasant life with the old woman who never said an angry word and gave her boiled or roast meat every day.

She stayed some time with Mother Holle, and then she became sad. At first she did not know what was the matter with her, but found at length that it was homesickness. Although she was many thousand times better off here than at home, still she had a longing to be there. At last she said to the old woman, "I have a longing for home. However well off I am down here, I cannot stay any longer. I must go up again to my own people."

Mother Holle said, "I am pleased that you long for your home again, and as you have served me truly, I myself will take you up again."

Thereupon she took her by the hand and led her to a large door. The door was opened, and just as the maiden was standing beneath the doorway, a heavy shower of golden rain fell. All the gold remained sticking to her, so that she was completely covered with it.

"You shall have this gold because you are so industrious," said Mother Holle. At the same time she gave the girl back the shuttle which she had let fall into the well. Thereupon the door closed, and the maiden found herself up above upon the earth, not far from her mother's house.

And as she went into the yard the cock was standing by the wellside and cried,

> *"Cock-a-doodle-doo!*
> *Your golden girl's come back to you!"*

So she went in to her mother, and because she arrived thus covered with gold, she was well received, both by her mother and her sister.

The girl told all that had happened to her, and as soon as the mother heard how she had come by so much wealth, she was very anxious to obtain the same good luck for the ugly and lazy daughter. She made her seat herself by the well and spin, and in order that the shuttle might be stained with blood, the girl stuck her hand into a thornbush and pricked her finger. Then she threw her shuttle into the well and jumped in after it.

The lazy daughter came, like the other, to the beautiful meadow and walked along the very same path. When she got to the oven the bread again cried, "Oh, take me out! Take me out or I shall burn. I have been baked a long time!"

But the lazy thing answered, "As if I had any wish to make myself dirty!" And on she went. Soon she came to the apple tree, which cried, "Oh, shake me! Shake me! We apples are all ripe!" But she answered, "One of you might fall on my head," and so went on.

When she came to Mother Holle's house she was not afraid, for she had already heard of her big teeth, and she hired herself to her immediately.

The first day she forced herself to work diligently and obeyed Mother Holle when she told her to do anything, for she was thinking of all the gold that she would give her. But on the second day she began to be lazy, and on the third day still more so, and then she would not get up in the morning at all. Neither did she make Mother Holle's bed as she ought, nor shake it so as to make the feathers fly up. Mother Holle was soon tired of this and gave her notice to leave. The lazy girl was willing enough to go and thought that now the golden rain would come. Mother Holle led her, too, to the great door, but while she was standing beneath it, instead of the gold a big kettle of tar was emptied over her.

"That is the reward of your service," said Mother Holle, and shut the door.

So the lazy girl went home, quite covered with tar, and the cock by the wellside, as soon as he saw her, cried out,

"Cock-a-doodle-do!
Your tarred girl's come back to you!"

The tar stuck fast to her, and could not be got off as long as she lived.

THE CRYSTAL BALL

HERE was once an enchantress who had three sons who loved one another dearly. The old woman, however, did not trust them and thought they wanted to steal her power from her. So she changed the eldest into an eagle which was forced to dwell in the rocky mountains and was often seen sweeping in great circles in the sky. The second she changed into a whale which lived in the deep sea, and all that was seen of it was that it sometimes spouted up a great jet of water in the air. Each of them only bore his human form for only two hours daily.

The third son, who thought she might change him into a raging wild beast, a bear perhaps, or a wolf, went secretly away. He had heard that a king's daughter, who was bewitched, was imprisoned in the Castle of the Golden Sun and was waiting for deliverance. Those, however, who tried to free her risked their lives. Three-and-twenty youths had already died a miserable death, and now only one other might make the attempt, after which no more must come. As his heart was without fear, he embraced the idea of seeking out the Castle of the Golden Sun.

He had already traveled about for a long time without

being able to find it, when he came by chance into a great forest and did not know the way out of it. All at once he saw in the distance two giants, who made a sign to him with their hands. When he came to them they said, "We are quarreling about a cap and which of us it is to belong to. As we are equally strong, neither of us can get the better of the other. The small men are cleverer than we are, so we will leave the decision to you."

"How can you dispute about an old cap?" said the youth.

"You do not know what properties it has! It is a wishing cap; whosoever puts it on can wish himself away wherever he likes, and in an instant he will be there."

"Give me the cap," said the youth. "I will go a short distance off, and when I call you, you must run a race. The cap shall belong to the one who gets to me first."

Then he put the cap on and went away. He thought of the king's daughter, forgot the giants, and walked continually onward. At length he sighed from the very bottom of his heart, and cried, "Ah, if I were but at the Castle of the Golden Sun!" Hardly had the words passed his lips than he was standing upon a high mountain before the gate of the castle.

He entered and went through all the rooms until in the last he found the king's daughter. But how shocked he was when he saw her. She had an ashen gray face full of wrinkles, dull eyes, and red hair.

"Are you the king's daughter, whose beauty the whole world praises?" cried he.

"Ah," she answered, "this is not my true form. Human eyes can only see me in this state of ugliness, but you may know what I am like. Look in the mirror. It does not let itself be misled, and it will show you my image as it is in truth."

She gave him the mirror in his hand, and he saw therein the likeness of the most beautiful maiden upon earth and saw, too, how the tears were rolling down her cheeks with grief. Then said he, "How can you be set free? I fear no danger."

She replied, "He who gets the crystal ball and holds it before the enchanter will destroy his power with it, and I shall resume my true shape. Ah," she added, "so many have already gone to meet death for this, and you are so young. I grieve that you should encounter such great danger."

"Nothing can keep me from doing it," said he, "but tell me what I must do."

"You shall know everything," said the king's daughter. "When you descend the mountain on which the castle stands, a wild bull will stand below by a spring, and you must fight with it. If you have the luck to kill it, a fiery bird will spring out of it. The bird bears in its body a burning egg, and in the egg the crystal ball lies like a yolk. The bird will not, however, let the egg fall until forced to do so. If the egg falls upon the ground, it will flame up and burn everything that is near and melt even ice itself, and with it the crystal ball, and then all your trouble will have been in vain."

The youth went down to the spring, where the bull snorted and bellowed at him. After a long struggle he plunged his sword in the animal's body, and it fell down. Instantly, a fiery bird arose from it and was about to fly away, but the young man's brother, the eagle, who was passing between the clouds, swooped down, hunted it away to the sea, and struck it with his beak until, in its plight, the fiery bird let the egg fall.

The egg did not, however, fall into the sea, but upon a fisherman's hut which stood on the shore. The hut began at once to smoke and was about to break out in flames. Then arose in the sea waves as high as a house. They streamed over the hut and subdued the fire. The other brother, the whale, had come swimming to them and had driven the water up on high. When the fire was extinguished, the youth sought for the egg and happily found it. It was not yet melted, but the shell was broken by being so suddenly cooled with the water, and he could take out the crystal ball unhurt.

When the youth went to the enchanter and held it before him, the latter said, "My power is destroyed, and from this time forth you are the king of the Castle of the Golden Sun. You can also give back to your brothers their human form."

Then the youth hastened to the king's daughter. When he entered the room, she was standing there in the full splendor of her beauty, and joyfully they exchanged rings with each other.